"Marry me."

Abby stared at Cade in disbelief. "Are you crazy?"

"Maybe," Cade said. "But Brandon needs two parents who love him."

He needs parents who love each other, Abby cried silently. "We can barely stand to be in the same room together," she argued.

"That's not what I'd call what was happening in the pool."

Abby's face heated. She couldn't deny that, not when she could still taste him on her lips. Gooseflesh rose on her skin, and she crossed her arms. Damn him. "We should try to have a cordial relationship—apart—except for raising our son."

"Brandon deserves more," Cade said. "He needs a mom and dad."

"I can't, Cade."

Cade watched as Abby ran into the house. His body still ached for her. Once again, his heart smarted from her rejection. But he wasn't going to let her push him away. Not this time. He was going to have his family.

A Child's Gift
Travis Comes Home

Dear Reader,

This June—traditionally the month of brides, weddings and the promise of love everlasting—Silhouette Romance also brings you the possibility of being a star! Check out the details of this special promotion in each of the six happily-ever-afters we have for you.

In *An Officer and a Princess,* Carla Cassidy's suspenseful conclusion to the bestselling series ROYALLY WED: THE STANBURYS, Princess Isabel calls on her former commanding officer to help rescue her missing father. Karen Rose Smith delights us with a struggling mom who refuses to fall for *Her Tycoon Boss* until the dynamic millionaire turns up the heat! In *A Child for Cade* by reader favorite Patricia Thayer, Cade Randall finds that his first love has kept a precious secret from him....

Talented author Alice Sharpe's latest offering, *The Baby Season,* tells of a dedicated career woman tempted by marriage and motherhood with a rugged rancher and his daughter. In *Blind-Date Bride*, the second book of Myrna Mackenzie's charming twin duo, the heroine asks a playboy billionaire to ward off the men sent by her matchmaking brothers. And a single mom decides to tell the man she has always loved that he has a son in Belinda Barnes's heartwarming tale, *The Littlest Wrangler.*

Next month be sure to return for two brand-new series— the exciting DESTINY, TEXAS by Teresa Southwick and the charming THE WEDDING LEGACY by Cara Colter. And don't forget the triumphant conclusion to Patricia Thayer's THE TEXAS BROTHERHOOD, along with three more wonderful stories!

Happy Reading!

Mary-Theresa Hussey

Mary-Theresa Hussey
Senior Editor

Please address questions and book requests to:
Silhouette Reader Service
U.S.: 3010 Walden Ave., P.O. Box 1325, Buffalo, NY 14269
Canadian: P.O. Box 609, Fort Erie, Ont. L2A 5X3

A Child for Cade

PATRICIA THAYER

THE TEXAS BROTHERHOOD

SILHOUETTE Romance

Published by Silhouette Books

America's Publisher of Contemporary Romance

To Steve, my friend, my lover, my computer expert.
As I write this, today is our anniversary, and it seems
only fitting that I dedicate this book to you. I want to
thank you for always being there with your love and
chocolate kisses. It's been a wonderful 30 years.
Forever yours, Pat.

 SILHOUETTE BOOKS

ISBN 0-373-19524-9

A CHILD FOR CADE

Copyright © 2001 by Patricia Wright

Visit Silhouette at www.eHarlequin.com

Printed in U.S.A.

Books by Patricia Thayer

Silhouette Romance

Just Maggie #895
Race to the Altar #1009
The Cowboy's Courtship #1064
Wildcat Wedding #1086
Reilly's Bride #1146
The Cowboy's Convenient Bride #1261
*Her Surprise Family #1394
*The Man, the Ring, the Wedding #1412
†Chance's Joy #1518
†A Child for Cade #1524

Silhouette Special Edition

Nothing Short of a Miracle #1116
Baby, Our Baby! #1225
*The Secret Millionaire #1252
Whose Baby Is This? #1335

*With These Rings
†The Texas Brotherhood

PATRICIA THAYER

has been writing for fourteen years and has published fourteen books with Silhouette. Her books have been nominated for the National Readers' Choice Award, Virginia Romance Writers of America's Holt Medallion and a prestigious RITA Award. In 1997 *Nothing Short of a Miracle* won the *Romantic Times Magazine* Reviewers' Choice Award for Best Special Edition.

Thanks to the understanding men in her life—her husband of thirty years, Steve, and her three sons—Pat has been able to fulfill her dream of writing romance. Another dream is to own a cabin in Colorado, where she can spend her days writing and her evenings with her favorite hero, Steve. She loves to hear from readers. You can write to her at P.O. Box 6251, Anaheim, CA 92816-0251.

SILHOUETTE MAKES YOU A STAR!
Feel like a star with Silhouette.
Look for the exciting details of our new contest
inside all of these fabulous Silhouette novels:

Chapter One

He never expected to see her here.

Cade Randell leaned against the post, oblivious to the sounds of the celebration going on around him. His only interest was the woman with the auburn hair and deep-green eyes standing across the patio. His body tensed as he examined her tall willowy frame. There was a hint of curves beneath the Indian-print skirt, the ivory T-shirt and honey-colored vest.

Damn, Abigail Moreau looked good. A dull pain gripped his chest at the realization that she hadn't been a Moreau for more than seven years. Not since she'd married Joel Garson.

Just then the woman looked in his direction. When their eyes met, her smile faded and was replaced with a panicked stare before she quickly glanced away.

Cade stiffened. He wasn't going to let her ignore him. He tipped his long-necked bottle against his lips and took a swallow of beer, then put the empty down on the table and went off to renew an old acquaintance.

He made his way through the crowd, his courage diminishing with each step.

Abby had never dreamed Cade Randell would return home, not after so many years. Her body trembled, and she wanted to run. But there was no escape. Cade had already seen her, and he looked determined to speak to her. She had known this day would come and had dreaded it. It had been nearly eight years. Enough time to forgive and forget and move on with their lives. That was it. He was probably just wanted to say hello.

The tallest of the three Randell brothers, Cade stood six-two. His body was long and lean with broad muscular shoulders. Dressed in black jeans, a wine-colored western shirt and polished sharkskin boots, he moved in a slow easy gait, as if he had all the time in the world. Abby drew another breath, trying to calm the wild beating of her heart.

He stopped in front of her. His face was as handsome as she remembered, but now there was a hard edge to his deep-set eyes. His short-cut raven hair still had a slight wave.

"Hello, Abby," he said in a deep baritone voice.

Another shiver raced through her. "Cade...it's good to see you." Her gaze locked with his night-brown eyes. The same incredibly beautiful eyes she'd seen every day for the past seven years. Her son's. Oh, God, she shouldn't have come tonight.

"Is it?" he asked.

She forced herself to look cheerful. "I'm sure Hank is happy you came back for his birthday celebration."

His stare grew more intense. "That's the only reason I came back. For Hank."

She didn't miss the anger in his voice. "He's a good man."

Cade nodded. "And the only person around San Angelo who'd take in three wild boys."

"Like I said, he's a good man."

"Speaking of men—" Cade glanced around "—I don't see your husband. Where is Joel?"

Abby tensed. No way was she going to explain her situation to Cade. "He's not here."

"What a shame. And here I wanted to give him my congratulations." His eyes bore into hers. "Let him know there are no hard feelings. Is he still working for his rich daddy?"

"Look, Cade, if you want to see Joel, you can contact him at the bank. He and I are no longer...married." Escape. She needed to get away. She started to leave, but Cade stepped in front of her.

"Why?" He had a cynical sneer on his face. "You were the perfect couple."

Abby fought the feeling of being trapped. "Nothing's perfect, Cade." She moved past him and made her way through the crowd. There was a clear path to the edge of the yard, but she wasn't fast enough.

Cade caught her. Taking her by the arm, he led her to a secluded area by some trees. "What happened, Abby?"

"It's really none of your business," she whispered, and tried to break his hold, but his grip only tightened.

"I think it is my business," he said. "Wasn't he enough for you, Abby? Couldn't he satisfy you, either?"

Suddenly Cade felt a weak push against his body,

then a stinging kick in the leg. "You leave my mom alone!" a child's voice cried out.

Cade released Abby and looked down to find a boy of about six or seven, pushing at him with all his might. He grabbed the child's arms and held him away before he could inflict any more pain. "Whoa, partner," Cade said. "I'm not hurting anyone. I was just talking to your mother."

The boy looked unconvinced. He jerked away, then hurried to Abby's side. So Abby had a child. Another pain stabbed his heart as he stared at the dark-haired boy.

"Brandon, it's all right," Abby said. "This is Cade, Chance's brother."

The boy glared at Cade, then at his mother. "But he grabbed you. Just like—"

"No, son. I'm okay," she assured him with a hug. "Why don't you go and play with your friends?"

"But, Mom…" Finally the boy nodded, gave Cade a warning look, then reluctantly wandered off.

Abby turned back to Cade. "I'm sorry, since the divorce, Brandon's been very protective of me."

Cade saw something in Abby's emerald eyes. Sadness? Fear? He felt a tightening in his chest again. Damn. Why should he care that her marriage broke up? She had made her choice years ago. And it wasn't him. Just walk away, Randell, he told himself. But he didn't move. "Why does your son think you need protection?"

Abby's back straightened and she raised her chin. "I don't need anyone's protection. I can take care of myself."

Before Cade could speak, his younger brother,

Travis, came over. "Cade, come on, we're going to toast Hank."

"Be there in a minute." He looked back at Abby. "We aren't finished with this conversation."

"Yes, we are, Cade," Abby said. "You've made a life in Chicago, and mine is here…with my son." She smiled, and it was as if something ripped the air from his lungs. Suddenly she was transformed into the same beautiful girl he'd once loved.

"Goodbye, Cade." She walked away.

"Come on, brother," Travis called again. "Chance is waiting for us at the bandstand."

"I'm coming." He looked over his shoulder to catch a final fleeting glimpse of Abby as she hurried off. Something told him it might be the last time he'd ever see her. He should be glad. If so, why was there a terrible ache in his gut?

Cade stood on the bandstand next to Hank, his brothers—Travis and Chance—and Chance's wife, Joy.

Nearly a hundred people had come to celebrate Hank Barrett's sixty-fifth birthday. A man who had been a rancher in the area all his life. A man who was loved and respected by all. A man who took in three wayward boys when everyone else had given up on them.

Cade's best childhood memories had been the years on the Circle B. It hadn't been an easy life, but Hank and Ella, the ranch housekeeper, were there for them. Besides his brothers, they were the only people Cade could depend on.

With a glass of champagne, Chance stepped to the microphone. "It's wonderful to see so many friends and neighbors here for Hank's birthday." He turned to Hank. "You know half these people came for the free food and beer," Chance teased, and everyone laughed. Cade watched his older brother in amazement. He'd never known Chance to joke around. He'd always been so serious about everything. Cade decided Joy and their new baby daughter had had a lot to do with it. Funny how love could change a person, Cade thought as he looked over the crowd while his brother continued to toast Hank.

Once again, his gaze wandered toward the back of the patio. Immediately he picked out Abby. When his eyes met hers, something stirred inside. Damn, he'd thought she'd headed home.

When Chance finished the toast, applause broke out, pulling Cade back to the reason he was here. It was his turn to step up to the mike.

"It's been nearly eight years," Cade began, "since the last time I was here at the Circle B. But Hank has welcomed me just as he did my brothers and me twenty years ago. Back then I was a smart-mouthed kid and thought I knew everything," he said as he glanced at Hank. The sixty-five-year-old rancher, with his head of thick gray hair, stood straight-backed. His face was weathered from the sun, but he'd retained his ready smile and kind heart.

"Hank told me I had a lot to learn. Then he proceeded to teach me how to muck out a stall, feed the livestock, brand a calf and shoe a horse. All skills I definitely needed in Chicago." The crowd laughed. Cade stole another glance at Hank, and he swallowed hard as his emotions threatened to erupt. "But the most valuable lesson I learned from this man was not to give up on a job, no matter how hard. He told me anything worth having is worth the struggle. It's what gives you such sweet satisfaction, knowing you've accomplished something.''

Cade raised his glass. ''To Hank. Thanks for all the lessons. And may your days all be sweet.'' There was silence as everyone took a drink, then unable to help it, Cade glanced at Abby again.

Abby knew she should have left when she had the chance, but this had been her first social outing since her daddy's death six months ago. Brandon needed the party, too. Since school let out, he'd been isolated from kids his own age. He'd been sticking close to her, playing her protector. But she didn't want him to worry about her. She wanted her son to be a kid. Tonight was for him. But was it safe to stay any longer?

When Cade stepped off the bandstand and headed toward her, Abby knew she had to get her son home where it was safe. Sending one of the teenagers to get Brandon, she planned to disappear before there were any more confrontations. No such luck. She looked up and saw Cade still moving in her direction. She tensed, ready for a fight.

He raised a calming hand. ''I just want to apologize for before. I had no right to talk to you that way.''

''No, you didn't,'' Abby said, though she knew after her rejection of him he had every right to despise her. He could never know that she hadn't had a choice. ''I know we never can be friends, Cade. But I do wish you the best. I hear you've made a good life for yourself in Chicago.''

He nodded. ''I have a job I like. I make a decent living.''

She'd known he would do well. ''You always worked hard. I'm glad everything's gone your way. I guess I better go. Goodbye, Cade.'' She made her way toward Brandon, fighting the urge not to turn around for one last look at the man she'd loved since the first day she saw him. No, Cade Randell was her past. She couldn't go back and change anything. It was too late, and there were too many secrets for him to forgive her.

Cade wasn't in a party mood anymore. He needed time alone. He headed toward the barn and some privacy. Damn, he didn't want these feelings for Abby stirred up. After all this time, he'd thought he could come back, no strings, just a nice visit with his brothers and Ella and Hank. No demons from his past. Cade walked down the center aisle and stroked a few of the horses in the stalls.

He'd left San Angelo and last seen Abby Moreau eight years ago. Now her hair hung to her chin, and was much tamer than the wild red mane that used to hang to the middle of her back. He groaned as memories of the silken strands draped over his body came rushing back. How she'd been able to make him forget all the cruelty in the world with just her touch. Then just as quickly he recalled Abby's parting words. *"It will never work between us, Cade,"* she'd said with tears in her eyes. *"I don't love you."*

"You were right, Abby," he said to himself. "We wouldn't have worked. Not when you wanted a man with money. And one without the last name of Randell."

"Hey, what are you doing out here by yourself?"

Cade swung around to see his older brother, Chance, coming toward him. "I'm not sure I know all those people anymore," he lied. The real reason was he didn't know if he fit in. Had he ever?

"Hell, the neighborhood hasn't changed that much. It's the same ranching families, though some of the kids have grown up. Got some pretty women here tonight."

"Whoa, better not let your wife hear you say that," Cade said, realizing his brother qualified as one of the lucky ones to have found Joy. Chance had also been the only one of the three brothers who stayed on the Circle B, totally content to ranch.

"Joy doesn't have to worry," Chance said. "She knows how I feel about her. I was thinking about you. All you and Travis have been doing these past years is working hard and making lots of money. Aren't you a millionaire yet?"

Cade glanced away. "A million doesn't seem to be enough these days, bro," he said. After all, Abby had come from money and chosen to marry into an affluent family, instead of marrying him.

"Took me a lot of years to learn that the right woman doesn't care," Chance said. "Not if she loves you."

"That's the key, Chance, but it never hurts to have the advantage of wealth."

"I noticed you had your eyes on a certain woman."

Cade looked at his boots. "Aren't I a little old for you to be checking up on me?"

"Just habit, I guess. It's hard not to watch over your younger brothers." Chance grinned and pushed his hat back, allowing his hair to fall across his forehead. "Can you believe how much Travis has changed?"

Cade shook his head. "Seems like he was just a skinny college student not that long ago. Now he has his own business." Travis and Chance looked more like brothers, Cade thought, the same sandy hair and light eyes like their mother. Cade had had the misfortune to inherit his daddy's dark looks.

"Travis seems to be here, but not here," Chance said, sobering. "There's something bothering him."

Cade smiled. "Yeah, probably trying to figure out how to spend all his money."

Chance shook his head. "I think it's more. He hasn't said more than two words since coming home. And that cell phone of his is attached to his ear. Tomorrow I'm going to get it and bury the thing. That way he'll be guaranteed a vacation."

Both brothers laughed.

"Abby looked good tonight," Chance said.

Cade knew his brother was fishing. Chance was the only one who knew about his past relationship with Abby Moreau. "History. It's best left there. Besides, I'll be gone in a few days."

"You have to go back that soon, huh?"

"I have clients who depend on me." That wasn't completely true. As a financial adviser, he could handle just about anything by phone or e-mail, but he didn't belong here anymore.

"You know, she divorced that jerk."

Cade didn't have to ask who Chance was talking about. "I'm not interested. She told me once that she didn't want me."

"Everyone makes mistakes, Cade. I think Abby's daddy was more interested in hooking his daughter up with Garson than she was."

"She had a choice."

"Well, whatever, she's had to pay a heavy price. I hear Joel was pretty free with his fists."

Cade's head jerked up. "You mean he hit her?"

"I'm not positive, but I heard stories, and I saw

Abby one time with bruises on her face. She told me she fell.''

Anger seethed through Cade. How could a man strike a woman? He thought back to earlier, how Abby had trembled when he touched her. Now he understood her son's reaction. Cade closed his eyes, trying to block out the pain. The pain he'd felt every day since she left him. But what kind of pain had Abby suffered?

"Tell Hank I'm going for a ride," he said. "I need to clear my head."

Chance patted him on the back. "Just remember I'm here if you need me."

Cade saddled up Gus, a big bay gelding. Chance had told him the horse would get him back to the barn if they got lost. Once on the open range, with the bright moonlight to guide the way, Cade gave Gus free rein and let him fly.

Twenty minutes later Cade reined in the animal at the edge of a rise, then wandered to a grove of trees by the creek. He climbed off and led Gus to the water's edge for a well-deserved drink. Cade sat down and looked out over the valley. Mustang Valley.

A place he and his brothers had come to a lot. Hank had told them stories about the wild horses who took refuge here because of the water and grazing land. Mostly because Hank didn't chase them off as a nuisance. Some people had labeled the Randell boys the same way. Like their cattle-rustling father who'd been sent off to prison, they were no good. Branded with the stigma of those circumstances and with their mother deceased, they had no one willing to take them in—until Hank Barrett.

It had taken Cade some time, but he'd finally realized how good Hank was to them. How he made the Randell brothers think they were worth something. That if you worked hard, people would see it. Cade had worked hard in school, then college. But he'd wanted to leave San Angelo, where the Randell name held too many bad memories. But he hadn't planned to go alone.

Abigail Moreau, the daughter of one of the richest men in the area, loved him. Cade's gaze went to the oak tree and the memory of their last day together came flooding back...

It had been a June afternoon, perfect for a ride to the valley. Cade had spread a blanket on the ground for them to sit on. He was nervous as he dug into his pocket, trying to find the small diamond he'd worked for months to buy. It wasn't a large stone, but it was all he could afford for now.

He looked at Abby and couldn't believe she loved him. She was so beautiful with her long red hair, tied back with a blue ribbon. He held up the ring, and her eyes grew bright with excitement.

"I love you, Abby. I want us to get married so you can go with me to Chicago. I know I don't have much now, just my college degree, but with my new job, I'll be able to take care of you. I know it's not what you're used to, but someday..."

"Oh, Cade." Abby blinked back the tears. "I love you, not what you have. Oh, yes, I'll be your wife."

Cade slipped the ring on, and she threw herself into his arms. He kissed her, then kissed her again, and soon they were lying on the blanket. He raised his head, trying to catch his breath. "I guess we better slow down."

Her gaze searched his face. "I don't want to stop, Cade. I want you to make love to me."

His heart jumped into his throat. "But, Abby, you said you wanted to wait…"

"I'm going to be your wife, Cade. I want to show you how much I love you…"

Cade shook his head to erase the memory. But he couldn't. He couldn't erase Abby's lie. She hadn't loved him. The next day his ring came back with a note, saying they were too young for marriage.

Cade got up and walked along the creek and thought back to the naive kid he'd been when he hadn't believed Abby's note and had gone to her house. It hadn't been until she told him to his face that he finally believed her. The clincher came a month later, when she married Joel Garson.

Cade picked up a flat rock and tossed it into the water. The last seven-plus years he'd worked day and night, driven because he hadn't been good enough for Abby Moreau. And now he had a successful career. Guess he could thank her for that. He was wealthy enough to buy and sell people like the Moreaus and Garsons. But none of that mattered, because what he really wanted he couldn't have. Abby. And it was too late, because he could never forgive her.

When Abby got home from the party, it was after eleven. By the time she got Brandon to bed, she was exhausted. But in the lonely silence of her old bedroom, sleep eluded her.

Abby went downstairs. Since her father's death, only she and Brandon lived in the big ranch house. It was almost eerie, with so many empty rooms. She stepped into her father's study, Tom Moreau's private domain, and flicked on the lights, then walked past the cinnamon-colored leather sofa and matching chair. The large mahogany desk sat facing French doors that opened onto a large flagstone patio adorned with white wrought-iron furniture. An olympic-size pool and an ornate fountain took up most of the yard, and multi-colored flowers and a boxwood hedge surrounded the property. Nothing had been too good for Tom Moreau. He had loved the lifestyle. Too bad he hadn't been able to pay for it.

Abby glanced over her shoulder at the pile of un-paid bills on the desk. In the past months she'd been trying to think of a way to pay off the debts. But with her limited financial knowledge, she hadn't come up with a single idea. She needed a professional, which she couldn't afford. But she also couldn't afford *not* to hire one. It was either that or she'd have to sell the ranch, her last resort. The Moreau ranch was Bran-don's legacy. Since the divorce, Abby knew this was all her son would have. And she'd do almost anything to keep her boy from losing it. She'd already used most of her divorce settlement paying the inheritance tax, then some more on the enormous debt, but it had hardly made a dent.

Joel wasn't about to help her, either. Besides, she didn't plan on taking anything else from her ex-husband. As it was, Joel practically made her beg for her monthly check. She guessed that it took the place of working her over with his fists.

Abby shivered and moved away from the window, hugging herself. Closing her eyes, she'd tried to erase the ugly memory of her marriage. A marriage her fa-ther had coerced her into.

Instead, she thought back to the day she'd gone to

Mustang Valley, the day Cade had asked her to marry him. She'd accepted quickly, unable to believe they were finally going to be together. They wouldn't have to hide any longer.

But Tom Moreau hated the Randells, ever since Cade's daddy had rustled his cattle. Abby knew he would fight her on the marriage, but never realized how far he'd go until that day.

Abby had arrived in the study with her new engagement ring. Her father was sitting behind his desk as usual. She was nearly twenty-two, and the man still frightened her. Well, she wasn't going to let her father control her life any longer. She wanted a life with Cade, and she was going to have it.

Her father stood. "You were with Randell."

Abby bit back a gasp. "I have a right to see whomever I please."

"I think not," he said. "You're a Moreau, and certain things are expected of you. You stay away from that trash."

"Cade isn't trash. He's a college graduate and has a good job in Chicago."

"Fine. Then he'll be out of here."

Abby grew braver. "And I'm going with him."

Her father looked her over and grinned. "I don't think so. I have plans for you."

"But I love Cade. We're getting married."

Tom sat on the edge of the desk. He looked calm, but Abby saw the anger in his eyes. "You know there's been more rustling going on in the area. I've lost several head myself. Two of the hands told me they saw someone who fits Cade Randell's description on the property."

Dread rushed over her. "It wasn't Cade."

"It's my word against a Randell. Who do you think people will believe?"

"That's not fair, you know Cade didn't do anything wrong."

"He did everything wrong when he touched Moreau property."

Abby flinched at the words. Was that all she was to him—his property? "Then I'll say he was with me. You won't be able to do anything. I'm of age. I can go away with Cade if I want."

She saw her father's jaw clench, then he drew a breath as if trying to gather his control. "You best not argue, girl."

Abby began to shake. "Daddy, please. I love Cade."

"If you love him, then you'll let him go. It's the only way he'll stay out of jail. Don't cross me, girl. Tomorrow you'll tell him you've made a mistake. Then I'm sending you off to Europe with the Garsons. Their son, Joel, asked about you." Her father smiled. "Now, there's a fine young man from a good family."

"I don't want to go out with Joel," she argued.

"I wasn't giving you a choice. That is, if you really care about Randell."

Abby knew she'd lost. "Okay, I'll go. But you have to promise me you'll leave Cade alone."

He glared at her, as if to say how dare she question him. Finally he nodded. "Send the ring back by messenger, I don't want you seeing Randell again."

For days Abby had ached to go to Cade and tell him the truth. But she knew her father would carry out his threats. The following week Abby was sent off to Europe with the Garsons. A month later when she returned home, her circumstances had changed. She was desperate to talk to Cade. But when she'd called him in Chicago, he didn't want to talk to her. He said their break up was for the best. They were too young to know about love. Brokenhearted, Abby had let herself be talked into marrying Joel.

Abby wiped the tears from her face. All these years, she'd never stopped loving Cade Randell. But there had never been a chance for them, not then, and certainly not now.

Not after he discovered her lies. Not after he discovered he had a son.

Chapter Two

The next morning Cade woke up groggy. He told himself it had been the excitement of the party, of returning home after all these years. He was staying in his old room. Things hadn't changed much, maybe a fresh coat of paint. The truth was, it had been Abby that robbed him of sleep.

By the time he showered and went downstairs, the family was already in the bright yellow kitchen eating breakfast. Hank sat at the head of the large trestle table, Cade's brothers, Chance and Travis, in the same places they had occupied years ago.

"Good morning." Cade took his seat.

"Well, it's about time you showed your face," Ella said, giving him a stern look, but her hazel eyes were smiling. The gray-haired woman was still housekeeper at the Circle B.

"Love you, too, Ella," Cade teased. He took a swallow of coffee from the mug she put in front of him. He sighed, waiting for the caffeine to kick in.

"Gotta get you accustomed to ranch life again," Hank said.

"In Chicago I'm usually up early because of the stock market."

"Must be Ella's cooking you're trying to avoid," Hank teased.

"Stop it, old man," Ella said. "Joy's been teaching me."

Cade chuckled, recalling that the Circle B's house-keeper had never been famous for her cooking. If she didn't burn the food, it was a good day. "As long as I don't have to eat my own cooking, it tastes good to me." He winked at Ella. "It was just a late night."

"Yeah, quite a party," Travis said with a smile that didn't reach his eyes. He quickly looked away to check the pager attached to his belt, then pulled out a cellular phone. He began punching the buttons as he got up from the table and walked into the pantry.

Cade watched his younger brother. There were only a few years' difference in their ages, but Travis had been in college when he'd left. Now, eight years later, his kid brother was nearly as big he was. And he ran his own company in Houston. Something to do with computer security. Funny, he didn't really know much about the business his brother had started. It must have been doing well. Travis's nice clothes and the Rolex on his wrist left little doubt. He had even brought Hank expensive gifts.

So it seemed all three of the Randells had made their way in the world. Too bad their worlds had to be so far apart.

"How was your ride last night?" Chance asked from across the table.

"Good," Cade said. "And there was plenty of moonlight to find my way back."

"Wish I'd known," Hank mumbled. "I would have gone with you. There were way too many people here to suit me. All that fuss over a silly birthday."

Ella set a plate of bacon and eggs in front of him. "If you'd left, Hank Barrett, I'd have skinned you alive."

"So would I."

They turned as Joy Randell walked into the kitchen, carrying her two-month-old daughter, Katie. The petite blonde crossed to Chance and gave him a lingering kiss, then handed him the baby. "She's been fed and changed."

"Hi, princess," Chance crooned to the child, and was rewarded with a smile.

Cade watched the loving exchange with envy. He was still amazed at their story. How Chance had met the widowed Joy Spencer in the abandoned barn of a neighbor. She'd been in labor, and he'd ended up delivering her baby. Not two weeks later, Chance had married her to keep the child from her in-laws. "Who would have thought it? My brother a family man."

Chance cocked an eyebrow at him. "Don't knock it, Cade. These two ladies are the best thing that ever happened to me."

"I didn't get a bad deal, either," Joy said as she sat down next to her husband, her bright blue eyes full of love.

Cade had thought that way once, too. His attention turned back to Abby and how beautiful she'd looked last night. She could still make his pulse race. But he knew better than to pursue it. She'd made a fool out of him once, and he wasn't going to play that game again. No, he'd stay away from Abby Garson.

Travis returned to the table, his expression even more troubled than before. "I need to get back to Houston. There's a problem…with one of our accounts."

"Can't your partner handle it?" Hank asked.

"No." Travis shook his head. "It's something I've got to do myself." He checked his watch. "I've got to get to the airport as soon as possible."

"I'll give you a ride, Trav," Cade volunteered. "At least we can visit awhile."

Travis nodded. "Thanks, Cade." He turned to Hank. "I'm sorry I have to cut this short. I promise to be back soon. Next time maybe I can stay longer."

Hank's eyes misted as he stood. "I'm gonna hold you to it, son." He hugged Travis.

Travis said his goodbyes to the rest of the family, then went upstairs to retrieve his bag. Cade headed outside and waited by the ranch truck. A few minutes later Travis came rushing out the door, along with Ella carrying a straw cowboy hat. "Cade, on your way back would you stop by the Moreau ranch and drop off this hat? Brandon left it here last night."

No way was he going near that place. Tom Moreau would probably shoot him on sight. "The kid probably has a lot of hats. He'll never miss it."

"He'll miss this one, though. His granddad gave it to him on his birthday—right before he died. Brandon never goes anywhere without it."

"Tom Moreau died?"

Ella nodded. "About six months ago. Cancer. It's been rough on Abby and that boy." She shoved the hat at him. "Now there's nothing there to scare you off. Or is there?"

Before Cade could answer, Ella hurried back into the house. "She's got something up her sleeve, and I don't like it," he muttered as he and Travis climbed into the cab.

Cade started the engine and took off down the road toward the highway. He glanced across the cab. "I hope there aren't any problems," he said, trying to get his brother talking.

His brother jerked his head around. "What?"

"I said, I hope there aren't any problems with your company."

Travis shrugged. "There're always problems."

Cade didn't like the sound of that. "Want to talk about it?"

Travis glared at him as he rested one booted foot across the other knee. "I'm not a kid anymore, Cade," he grumbled.

"Whoa there." Cade held up a hand. "I was only offering some help. If you don't want to talk, fine. I'll butt out. I just wanted you to know that I'm here if you need me."

"I don't think you would say that if you knew… Never mind." Travis head jerked to the side window.

Cade didn't want to "never mind." He had a strong feeling his brother was in trouble. "So you're going to be too stubborn to ask for help?"

Travis released a long sigh. "Hell, I can ask for all the help in the world, but it isn't going to bail me out of this."

Cade knew he couldn't force Travis to talk about it, and the rest of the trip passed in silence. When they arrived at the airport, Travis was practically out of the truck before it stopped. But Cade had to give it one more try. Opening the door, he stood and rested his arm on the door frame. "Hey, Trav, call me if you need anything."

Duffel bag in hand, Travis turned back to him and shook his head. "No, I don't want the family involved in this."

He looked so sad, so alone, Cade nearly went after him. "Whatever it is, it can't be that bad." He prayed his words were true. "Please, Trav, let me help."

They looked at each other for a long time. "It's bad. Just like it was with dad," Travis said, then disappeared through the terminal entrance.

Cade knew the way to the Moreau ranch blindfolded. Not that he was ever allowed on the property, but he'd ridden by on horseback so many times he'd lost count. He'd always been hoping to catch a glimpse of Abby.

Cade drove the truck under the wrought-iron archway that read "Moreau Cattle Ranch." He knew it had been one of the biggest operations in the area. Tom Moreau had other businesses besides cattle. He owned sheep and several pecan orchards, plus a few other properties.

No wonder the man hadn't wanted his daughter to hook up with the likes of him—a Randell. If only he'd given Cade a few years to prove himself. But Abby hadn't been willing to wait around for that, either.

Cade caught sight of the large brick home with its white wood columns along the porch supporting a second-story balcony. He parked the truck and grabbed the cowboy hat off the seat and climbed out. Maybe if he just left it by the door someone would find it.

Quit acting like a coward, he told himself. *You don't have to sneak around anymore.*

As he approached the house, he noticed the peeling paint on the porch and shutters. He turned toward the other buildings. They could all use a fresh coat of paint. To his surprise, no one had come out to ask what he was doing on Moreau property.

He shook his head. No, this wasn't his business, he told himself as he marched up to the porch and rang the bell. He was just going to drop off the hat and leave. But his plans changed when the door opened and a heavyset woman clutched his arm and tugged him inside.

"It's about time you got here," she scolded. "Ms. Abby has been waiting for you. Now go into the study and wait." She motioned him into a room that Cade realized must have been Tom Moreau's study.

Cade grinned. "Well, I'll be damned." He glanced at the portrait of the powerful rancher that hung above the used-brick fireplace. "Never could get over yourself, could you, Tom?"

It had taken Cade a long time, but men like Tom Moreau no longer intimidated him. He'd learned the hard way that if you had money, you had power, and you could play with the big boys.

Cade wandered over to the desk, the only place in the room that wasn't in order. Curiosity got the better of him, and he glanced at some of the papers. Overdue bills seemed to make up one stack. On a notepad was the name Ted Javor, Accountant.

"What are you doing here?"

Cade refused to look guilty when he turned around.

At the sight of Abby, he found he had trouble concentrating for other reasons. Her hair was pulled behind her ears, her face devoid of makeup, and he could see the light dusting of freckles across her nose and cheeks. A pair of worn jeans covered her long slender legs and cupped her shapely hips. Her fitted white blouse showed off more than a hint of her full breasts. Damn, Abby Moreau, you definitely filled out.

"I was invited in," he said. "In fact, your house-keeper practically pushed me in here."

Abby looked unconvinced. "Carmen let you in? That's hard to believe."

"You can believe what you want. I'm only here because your son left this at the party." He held out the cowboy hat.

"Oh," she said, and some of the fire died from her eyes. She took it from him. "Well, thank you for bringing it by." She folded her arms across her chest as if refusing to offer him any neighbourly niceties.

"Look, Cade, I'm too busy to stop and try to make small talk. You don't want to do that with me any more than I do with you. You made that clear last night." To his surprise she turned to leave.

"That wasn't always true," he said. "It was your decision…years ago."

Her eyes flashed again. "I think you've overstayed your welcome."

Cade knew he'd pushed too hard. "Wait, Abby. That was uncalled for. What I wanted to say is that I'm sorry about your daddy. I just heard about his passing."

Abby didn't need to deal with Cade Randell today, or ever. The man she saw last night and again this morning held no resemblance to the man she'd known so long ago. There was a hard edge to this Cade. He had the look of someone you didn't want to cross. If he ever discovered the truth… Thank goodness the foreman had taken Brandon along on his errands.

"Thank you," she said.

"Are you and Brandon getting along okay?"

Abby stared at him, surprised that he seemed concerned. "We're fine."

"I mean since the divorce and all. This is a big ranch for you to run by yourself."

She didn't want to discuss her problems with him. "I have help here," she lied. Most of the ranch hands were gone now. All she could afford to keep on was Charlie and his wife, Carmen. Carmen said Abby and Brandon needed her, and she couldn't leave without her husband anyway.

"I couldn't help but notice the place seems deserted," Cade said. His dark gaze bore into hers until she had to look away.

"My father was downsizing the cattle operation the last few years." That was all she was going to admit to the man. "Look, Cade, I really am busy. I'm expecting someone."

"An accountant?" he said.

She froze. "How did you know?"

"I expect your housekeeper thought I was him. She didn't give me a chance to tell her any differently, and then I couldn't help noticing what was on the desk. And Ted Javor's name on the notepad." He tossed her a grin, and for a second he reminded her of the boy she once knew. Feeling warmth spread through her, she realized her body was remembering, too.

Oh, God. She couldn't do this. "Thanks again for bringing the hat by." She walked to the door, hoping Cade would follow. He did, but stopped in the doorway and leaned toward her. He was close enough that

she could see he had nicked himself shaving. Slowly
her gaze raised to his, finding the golden flecks in the
dark depths of his eyes, framed with long black lashes.

"If you're having a rough time, Abby, I might be
able to help. I'm a financial adviser."

She stiffened. "I'm fine. And I'm more than capa-
ble of running the ranch."

He started to say something, but nodded, instead.
"Goodbye, Abby. I won't bother you again." He
walked out, and she prayed that he was telling her the
truth, because she didn't think she could handle seeing
Cade Randell again.

Back at the Circle B by early afternoon, Cade
parked the truck outside the corral with plans of opening a beer and sitting around being lazy the rest of the
day. Hell, it was his vacation. The first he'd taken in
years. He didn't need any more headaches from his
brother or a woman from the past.

As he started for the house, he heard hollering from
the barn and decided to see what all the commotion
was about. Inside he found Chance and Hank by a
stall, eyeing the latest addition to the ranch. A new
chestnut filly.

Cade came closer and to his surprise he found Brandon Garson standing alongside Hank. For the first time
Cade had a chance to see Brandon when the boy
wasn't scowling. He was a good-looking kid with dark
wavy hair and big brown eyes. Maybe a little on the
thin side. Cade smiled. Something about Brandon reminded him of Travis.

"Cade, you missed it," Hank said. "Lady dropped
her foal just after you left this morning."

"I can see that." He stepped closer to the stall and

noticed Brandon move back. Was the boy afraid of him? He remembered what Chance had said about Joel's treatment of Abby. Had he mistreated the boy, as well? Cade tensed, recalling his own daddy's free-swinging backhand. It had taken a long time for Cade to trust other adults. He wasn't sure why, but it was important he get Brandon to trust him.

"Brandon, she's pretty cool, huh?" Cade asked.

The boy remained silent.

That didn't stop Cade. "If I'd known you were going to stop by, I wouldn't have taken your hat to your house."

Brandon finally looked at Cade. "My hat?"

"Yes, Ella found it and said it was real special because your granddad gave it to you. So I ran it over to your place."

The boy's dark eyes turned hostile. "Did you see my mom?"

"Yeah, but she was too busy to talk." He shrugged. "So I left."

"Oh," was all Brandon said.

Cade wasn't getting very far. He turned to Hank. "What are you going to name the foal?"

"Not sure," Hank said as he took off his hat and scratched his head. "I've named so many over the years I think I've run out."

Cade studied the new filly. "What about you, Brandon? You got any ideas you can give Hank and Chance?"

"I don't know." The boy shrugged his narrow shoulders. Then he glanced up at the men towering over him, his eyes bright. "Maybe you could call her Princess Star. Princess for what Chance always calls his little girl and because the foal has a star on her forehead." The boy immediately ducked his head and peeked back at the horses.

Cade watched as Hank and Chance exchanged a smile. "Hey, Brandon," Chance said. "I think that's a mighty fine name. When Katie gets a little older, I bet she'll like it, too."

"Then it's okay?" the boy asked.

"It's more than okay," Hank agreed. "It's great."

Brandon's face broke into a grin as Hank ruffled his hair. Something tightened in Cade's chest as he watched the happy exchange. He found he wanted to get the same reaction from the boy.

The group broke up as the men started off toward corral. The Moreau-ranch foreman, Charlie, instructed Brandon to stay close to the stall.

"I'll keep an eye on him," Cade offered.

When they were alone, Cade still kept his distance. He knew that he and the boy had gotten off on the wrong foot, and he needed to set him straight about a few things. "You know, Brandon, I used to go to school with your mom."

The boy didn't react.

"In fact, I had a crush on her. I thought she was the prettiest girl in school."

"She's still pretty," Brandon said.

Cade smiled. "Yes, she is." He knelt down on one knee next to the child. "And I want you to know I would never do anything to hurt her. I was wrong to grab her arm last night. And I told her today I was sorry."

Brandon still didn't look at him. "My dad used to say he was sorry a lot. But he didn't mean it."

Cade tried to remain calm. If he ever got his hands on Joel Garson... "Well, I'm not like your dad. Hank raised me to respect women. That's the reason when I got out of line last night, I apologized to your mom. But I swear I have never ever hit a woman. Only cowards do that.''

Brandon turned to him, his eyes guarded as they examined him closely. ''Did you really live here?''

''Yeah, after my daddy went…away.''

''My grandpa said your daddy rustled cattle and went to prison. And you and your brothers were no good, either.''

Why would Tom Moreau be talking about his family? ''Just because your daddy did bad things, does that mean you will, too?''

Brandon shook his head. ''No.''

''Well, it's the same with me. I went to college and then got a good job in Chicago. And I guarantee you I never rustled any cattle.''

The boy finally smiled, showing off the space from a missing front tooth. ''Do you have a ranch there?''

''No, no ranches there, but I have a house. Chicago is a big city. I work on the twenty-seventh floor of a very tall building.

''Oh. Don't you miss it here?''

''Sometimes. I miss my brothers and Hank and riding horses all the time. I even miss my secret hiding place.''

The boy's eyes rounded. ''You have a secret hiding place?''

''Doesn't everyone?''

''I have one at my grandpa's ranch,'' he said. ''Will you show me yours?''

Cade grinned. ''Well, I don't know. It wouldn't be a secret hiding place if I showed it to you.''

''I won't tell anyone, promise.''

"Double-spit-swear?"

Brandon looked confused. "I don't know what that means."

Cade stood, trying to remember how he and his brothers used to do the ritual. He raised his hands, spit into each palm, wiped them on his jeans, then made a cross over his heart. "Double-spit-swear."

He watched in amazement as Brandon followed suit and looked up proudly. "Now can you show me?"

"Guess I'm gonna have to." Cade started off toward the front of the barn, but before he got very far, he saw Abby come rushing in.

"Brandon," she called.

"Hey, Mom." The boy ran to her. "Did you come to see Hank's new filly? I got to name her—Princess Star."

She hugged Brandon to her side. "That's nice, son, but we need to be getting home."

Abby finally glanced at Cade. She was still wearing her jeans and boots. Her hair wasn't as tame as last night. He liked it better this way.

"Hi, Abby."

"Cade."

"You should take a look at the new filly," Cade said.

"Yeah, Mom. She's real pretty." Brandon tugged on her arm until she followed him to the stall.

Abby didn't want this. Brandon and Cade couldn't be together. She'd had no idea Charlie was going to bring her son to the Circle B when he said he had errands to run. She'd panicked when Carmen told her.

Cade came up beside her, standing so close she could feel his heat. She could smell him. No fancy colognes, just soap and the intoxicating scent of the man himself.

"She's pretty," Abby said, and stepped away from Cade. "Okay, son, why don't you say goodbye and we'll leave."

"But why can't I stay until Charlie goes back? Cade was going to show me his secret hiding place." Brandon slapped his hand over his mouth. "Sorry, I didn't mean to tell her."

"That's okay." Cade ruffled Brandon's hair. "She doesn't know where it is."

Abby knew all about secret places. Cade and she had shared one a long time ago. "You weren't going to take him out to the valley, were you?"

Cade shook his head, then a smile appeared. "So you remember?"

She glanced away. How could she forget? Her son had been conceived there. And she had to keep that secret. "Some other time, Brandon. Let's go." She took his hand.

Just then Hank walked in with Charlie.

"Well, hello, Abby," Hank said. "What a pleasure to see you again."

"Hello, Hank," she said. "I'm sorry we intruded on your workday."

"Glad you did. Charlie helped Chance load up two mares to take back to his ranch."

"Did you need me, Abby?" the foreman asked.

"No, I just thought I'd take Brandon home. I don't want him to get underfoot."

"He's never that," Hank said. "He was a big help today. Besides, I enjoy having him here." He eyed Cade. "My boys are all grown-up."

"You're very kind, Hank. We'll just head home now."

"I got an idea," the old rancher said. "Stay for supper. We've got tons of leftovers from the party. Charlie, you call Carmen and have her come, too."

Before Abby could stop him, Hank had wandered off. Great, now she had to spend the evening here. How was she going to keep Cade and Brandon apart?

"Looks like you both are staying," Cade said. "You want to come with us to my secret hiding place, Abby?" He cocked a dark eyebrow. "But first I got to double-spit-swear you to secrecy."

"Yeah, Mom. It's gonna be cool."

She knew she should refuse to let Brandon go, but that might raise suspicions. More regrets flooded her as once again she questioned her decision years ago. "I think I'll pass. I'll just go to the house and see if I can help Ella with supper."

"Too, bad." He grinned, then looked at Brandon. "Looks like it's just us guys, huh, son?"

Abby's heart pounded.

"All right," Brandon said.

"Be careful, Cade," Abby said. "He's just a child."

Cade leaned toward her and whispered, "It's only an old storage shed out back. In case you're interested in finding us, it's past the oak tree with the swing. Come on, Brandon. Let's go see if my treasure box is still there."

Abby watched the two walk off together. Did any-one else see the resemblance? The dark hair and set eyes. Even their gaits were similar. Oh, God
was she going to keep Cade from finding ou
would it be fair to?

* * *

They ate dinner in the kitchen at the large table. Just like one big happy family. Abby listened to the laughter and many stories. Brandon had always been relaxed around Hank and Ella. Now it seemed that Cade was his new best friend.

Then there were the quick glances Cade tossed at her. He made her nervous. And it wasn't just because he was Brandon's father. Why was he suddenly flirting with her when last night he acted as if he couldn't stand the sight of her?

Cade knew he was playing with fire. He ought to steer clear of Abby, but he couldn't seem to manage it. She still stirred his desires whenever she was around. He told himself it was natural because they had a past together. She had been his first love.

While the women cleared the table, Hank invited Brandon into his study for a game of checkers. Cade excused himself and went out to the porch. He sat with his coffee and enjoyed the sunset, golden and orange as the sun dipped behind the trees. Had the sunsets here always been so beautiful?

Now he sat in the absolute stillness, eyes closed, listening to the sounds around him. Off in the distance, a horse whinnied and a dog barked. He'd thought the quiet would drive him crazy, but in the past three days it only seemed to relax him.

"Cade?"

He opened his eyes to see Abby. Suddenly his pulse began to race again. Damn. Get over it. She's just a woman. A woman who rejected you.

"Ella thought you'd like a piece of apple pie."

"Thanks," he said, and took the plate she offered. She started to walk away.

"Aren't you having any?" he asked.

"No, I ate too much at dinner."

"Don't tell me you're one of those women who diets all the time."

She straightened. "No, I'm just too full to eat any more. I'll take my dessert home." She started for the door again.

"Sit down and talk to me."

"Cade, I don't think that's a good idea."

"I told Brandon we used to be friends in school. I don't want him to think there's any hostility between us."

"In other words you want us to lie."

Cade put down his pie and stood. He went to her, took her hand and tugged her back to the porch. "I want us to act civil, Abby. I know we have some baggage from the past, but I'm only going to be around a few more days. Can't we get along?"

Abby pulled her hand away. "Sure. When are you going back?"

"The end of the week."

She walked to the railing. "Being here must be boring compared to Chicago."

Watching her face, he felt his heart trip. The dusky light highlighted her hair like a halo. Damn, being this close to her was killing him.

"No, not really," he said. "In fact, I've been enjoying my stay. I'm glad we got a chance to see each other again. Maybe clearing the air was a good thing. I'd like to put the past behind us and move on."

She shrugged. "Cade, I put our past away long ago."

She was lying. He could see it in her eyes. Or

maybe it was just wishful thinking that Abby Moreau Garson still had some feelings for him.

"Let's just test that theory." He drew her into his arms and covered her mouth with his. He heard her sharp intake of breath. But it didn't take long before her arms circled his neck, and she surrendered to the desire he knew now they would always share.

Then the bliss suddenly ended when Abby tore her mouth from his with a soft cry. Her eyes met his, and Cade could see a mixture of pain and longing in their emerald depths. Then Abby turned and dashed into the house.

Chapter Three

It had been a stupid thing to do.

The next morning Abby was still chastising herself for letting Cade kiss her. As if she'd had a choice. Whenever the man got within ten feet of her, she turned to mush. And she had to stop it, she told herself as she paced her bedroom. She wasn't a crazy-in-love college student any longer. She was a single mother, trying to raise her child. Cade's child. Just the thought turned her legs to jelly. She sank onto the bed. If he discovered Brandon was his...

Abby quickly shook away the thought. Cade would be gone by the end of the week. Just as before, Chicago was where he wanted to be. He'd proved that when he'd stayed away from San Angelo for so long, never interested in her well-being or if she could be pregnant from their lovemaking.

Tears started to well up in her eyes, but Abby refused to let them fall. She wasn't going to waste her time on something that could never be. Her only concern was her son. She wanted to protect him and to raise him with love in a good home.

That was one of her other problems. One she'd been dreading all week but couldn't put off any longer. Damn her ex-husband for doing this to her, for humiliating her this way. Obviously if she wanted her alimony check, she'd have to play Joel's game.

She dressed in a pair of pleated taupe slacks and a cream-colored blouse. After slipping on a pair of nut-brown flats, she went downstairs. She checked her hair in the mirror, then turned to find her son watching her.

"Where are you going, Mom?"

"Into town, honey. You stay with Charlie and Carmen."

"Can I go with you?"

"No, I'm going to the bank to see your fa—Joel. I'll be back soon, I promise."

She didn't miss the fear in his eyes as he shook his head. "No, Mom, don't go."

"I have to, Brandon. He didn't send the check."

"But what if he hurts you again?"

Abby forced a smile. "He won't, Brandon. That's why I'm going to the bank. There'll be a lot of people around. I'll be fine." She kissed him, then hurried out to her car, remembering that her therapist had told her to confront her fears. Abby seriously doubted that the psychologist realized what it was like to be knocked around by a drunken Joel Garson.

Cade drove into town, amazed at how things had changed. But after nearly eight years, what did he expect? Nothing stays the same. Before he knew it, his thoughts had turned to Abby. She had only become more beautiful with the years.

No. He had to stop thinking about her, Cade told himself as he pulled the truck into the First Security Bank parking lot. The kiss had been out of line, but it only verified what he already knew. Abby could still turn him inside out. Four more days, and he'd be back in Chicago. Back to his life with no Abby Garson to tempt him. He climbed out and walked into the one-story brick building. It was Tuesday, and the bank was quiet. Three tellers handled the customers. Cade pulled out the deposit slip and check Hank had given him and got in line.

He was next when he heard a loud voice that echoed through the hollow building. Cade glanced toward the glass enclosure. His heart pounded harder when he saw Abby inside—with Joel.

He froze when he saw that Garson had a grip on her wrist. The average person not looking closely wouldn't see the man's intense look. Fury raced through Cade as he made his way across the bank. What did Abby think she was doing, going to see Joel on her own? The man had beaten her before. He could do it again. If Garson touched her, he would be a dead man.

A receptionist looked up as he approached the door. "You can't go in there, sir."

"The hell I can't." Cade gave the door a sharp knock, then swung the door open to see Joel corraling Abby, his hand still gripping her wrist.

"Garson!" he growled.

The big stocky man turned to him in surprise. Joel Garson hadn't aged well. He had the ruddy complexion and puffy eyes of a drinker. He looked as if he'd been on a weekend binge. His stomach hung over his belt, and not even a custom-made suit could hide the fact that he was a good thirty pounds overweight.

"Release Abby or I'll break you in two." Cade stepped inside, then shut the door. He gripped the doorknob so he wouldn't carry out his threat.

Joel glared at him. "Get out, Randell. This is between my wife and me."

"Your *ex*-wife." Cade pushed away from the door, his fists clenched. "Let her go."

Abby remained silent, but her eyes revealed her panic.

"Now." Cade growled.

Finally Joel dropped Abby's wrist and backed away. "You'll be sorry you interfered in something that isn't any of your business."

"Yeah, I'm real scared," Cade said. "I doubt you would go at it with someone your own size."

"You can go to hell."

"Not before you give Abby what she came for."

Another glare, and Joel finally walked around the desk and opened the drawer. He pulled out an envelope and shoved it at her.

Abby's hand trembled as she took it. Then she moved away. Cade opened the door, but turned back to Joel. "If you want a fight, Garson, I'll gladly accommodate you. Just leave Abby alone."

"You'll be sorry for this, Randell."

"Never. Just don't let me hear that you hassled her again."

Cade shut the door and caught up with Abby. With a protective hand at her back, he escorted her through the bank, past the curious glances of several onlookers. He felt her stumble. His arm went around her waist, pulling her against his side. "It's okay, darlin', we're nearly out of here," he whispered. "Just hold it together a little while longer."

Finally outside, she sucked in a long breath, but it didn't bring much color back to her face.

"Come on, you need to sit down." He led her to the coffee shop next door and Cade directed her to a booth, then ordered two cups of coffee from the waitress.

He turned his attention to Abby. "Are you okay?"

She took a swallow of water. "No, I'm humiliated. How could you storm in there like that?"

"Look, I could hear Garson's voice from across the bank," he said, wondering where her gratitude was. "Did you want me to wait until he started smacking you around?"

She covered her face with her hands.

Cade ached to hold her, but figured she wouldn't welcome a man's touch right now. "How long has Joel been abusing you?"

She gasped at the question. "How…"

"Chance told me his suspicions." Cade couldn't hide his anger over the situation. "Brandon's actions confirmed it. How long did you put up with the man beating you?"

"This is none of your business."

"I'm sorry, Abby. I only want to help."

"Well, you're not. I have to deal with Joel." Her eyes filled with tears, and the sight broke his heart.

Even remembering the pain she'd caused him, Cade had the overpowering urge to protect her. He reached out and took her hand. "Abby, you don't have to take anything from the man. You don't even have to see him."

"I do. It's the only way I can get my money."

"Then go to court. Tell the judge what he's doing."

She pulled her hand away. "I can't, at least not now."

"Abby, you can't let Joel get away with this."

She gave him a jerky nod. "I know."

"Promise me you'll go back to court."

"I can't promise you anything, I don't have the money. Are you satisfied now? I'm broke."

The waitress suddenly appeared with the coffee, and Abby's face reddened. Cade wasn't surprised by her confession. He'd seen the shape of the ranch and that stack of unpaid bills on her desk.

She finally looked at him again. "How did you know I was at the bank?"

"I didn't. I was handling some business for Hank. It's a good thing I was there."

Abby closed her eyes, but not before he saw her pain. "I've got to get home," she said.

He wanted to help her. "Wait, Abby. You're not in any shape to drive."

She sighed. "Look, Cade, I'm fine. What I need now is to get back to my son. Thanks for what you did, but I can handle things on my own." She stood, squared her shoulders and walked out of the restaurant.

Well, she sure told him. Cade tried not to feel hurt over Abby's rejection. But once again she'd walked away from him.

She had made a mess of everything.

Abby sat at the desk in her father's study. After yesterday's events had robbed her of sleep, she'd gotten up before 5:00 a.m. She'd gone out and helped Charlie feed the stock, then returned to the house and showered. Now she was trying to sort through the mound of bills. Her support check hadn't gone far to help the situation, but at least they wouldn't starve.

Her son was getting the worst of the deal. He was going to lose his inheritance—the Moreau ranch. Her thoughts turned to Cade and what had happened at the bank. Damn. She didn't want the man championing her. It had taken her five years to get out of a loveless marriage and months of therapy to make her strong enough to handle her life. But Cade Randell wasn't just any man. He was her son's father.

The sound of the doorbell interrupted her, along with Brandon scurrying across the hardwood floors, yelling he would get it. More commotion when her son walked into the study with Cade in tow. Her heart pounded in panic and she rose to her feet.

"Hey, Mom, look! Cade's here. He said he had something for me."

Abby hadn't seen her son smile so much in months. "He did?"

She glanced at Cade. He looked wonderful. Since returning home, he'd dressed in slim-fitting jeans with a stacked hem on hand-tooled boots. A tan western shirt showed off his broad shoulders. She raised her gaze to his face, to his mouth. Heat surged through her as she recalled their searing kiss.

She quickly looked away. "You didn't need to bring Brandon a gift."

"It's nothing much." Cade pulled out an aged leather pouch and opened it. "I found these Indian arrowheads in a box in my old room. I thought Brandon would like them."

Brandon came closer to see. "Wow! These are cool." He picked one up. "Where did you get them?"

"My brothers and I used to collect them. We'd ride

out to Mustang Valley. All along the creek there are a lot of them.''

Abby knew that was true. She'd found some, too, when she'd ridden out to meet Cade.

''Can I go out there sometime with you?''

Abby wanted to scream no, but managed to bite back her objection.

Cade placed his hand on the child's shoulder. ''It's a long ride.'' His dark gaze met Abby's. ''We'll see.''

Brandon didn't hide his disappointment. ''That's what everybody says.''

''Brandon, that's not a nice way to act,'' Abby said.

The boy looked at Cade. ''Sorry. Thank you for the arrowheads.''

''You're welcome.''

Cade knew that all the things that had happened to him recently must have been rough on the kid.

''How about I take you riding sometime? If it's okay with your mom.''

The boy's eyes lit up. ''Really? You mean it? Mom, can I go?''

Cade knew he'd put Abby on the spot, but he wanted to help. And she wasn't about to let him without putting up a fight. He was crazy. A few more days and he'd be back in Chicago. Abby would be a part of his past again. Could it hurt if he spent some time with her and her son? He was smart enough to know that nothing would come of it. All he had to do was resist the urge to kiss her again.

''If you stay close to the house.'' She turned to Cade. ''He just started riding with my dad before... He hasn't had much time on horseback.''

''That's because we lived in town,'' Brandon said. ''But I have my own horse, Smoky—she's a mare—

and my grandpa gave me his horse, too. But I can't ride him until I'm bigger. I'm gonna go show Charlie my arrowheads. I'll be back." The boy ran out of the room before either adult could stop him.

Cade shook his head. "Where does he get that energy?"

"He's always had it. I used to have trouble getting him to quiet down…"

"And Joel didn't like that," Cade finished for her. "Good Lord, didn't the man realize what a great kid Brandon was?"

Ignoring his comment, Abby said, "I don't want to keep you, Cade. I'm sure you have better things to do. Like spending time with Hank."

"Hank's off to the cattle auction this morning," he said. "I came by to see if I could help you."

"Help me?"

"I work in finance, Abby. There might be something I can do to help with your…situation."

Her stubborn chin came up. "There's nothing anyone can do. I've already paid an accountant to tell me my best solution is to sell the ranch."

"What would it hurt to get a second opinion?"

She stared at him, unbelieving.

"I already know that you're in financial trouble, Abby. I promise you I'll handle everything discreetly. Nothing will leave this room."

Abby blinked. Cade would be here…with Brandon. But what if he really could help her? She couldn't turn down the chance to save the ranch. They wouldn't have to move back into town, and she wouldn't have to go to work full-time in town somewhere. The last thing she wanted was for her son to be a latchkey kid.

She'd grown up without a mother and didn't want that for her son. Brandon needed to grow up on the ranch.

"I guess it wouldn't hurt," she conceded.

Cade released a long breath. "Okay, lead me to the files."

Abby directed him to the desk. "All the files are in the drawers." She pulled out the ranch ledger and handed it to him.

Within ten minutes Cade was deeply engrossed in the job. Not seeing any reason to stay around, Abby left, praying that Cade could come up with some ideas how to help. Her son and the ranch were all she had. She would never take another chance on love again.

After a few hours Cade realized that Abby hadn't exaggerated the situation. Things were bleak. Several times he'd cursed Tom Moreau and his poor judgment, his inability to conserve when cattle prices took a dive.

Now all Cade had to do was come up with a miracle. The short-term solution for Abby was to sell off most of the herd to come up with some quick cash to cover debts.

Long term, she had to make the ranch profitable again. Not an easy task, since it would take a few years to get things going again. Besides cattle, Abby needed another way to make her land pay. She might have to sell some acreage to get things started, such as the valuable lake property. Cade had a few other ideas, but he wanted to discuss them with Hank and Chance first.

Before he realized it, the afternoon had flown by. Carmen had brought him lunch which he'd eaten while working. He should probably head home. He got up and was closing the folders when Abby walked in.

"Are you finished?"

"No. I just went over the ranch records. This place hasn't been working at a profit for the past few years."

"I know that now, but not when Dad was alive," she admitted. "He never confided in me about business."

Cade saw the forlorn look in Abby's eyes. Again he felt the urge to pull her into his arms. But he knew that would only lead to trouble. Trouble he didn't need, like the kiss they'd shared the other night. He let his gaze fall to her mouth, recalling her taste, her softness, and his pulse began to race. All at once he realized what he was doing, and he forced himself to return to business.

"I don't know if there was anything you could have done. My big concern is the bank note. Did you know that Joel can foreclose on you by the first of next month?"

She nodded. "Believe me, it's something he doesn't let me forget."

Cade was worried. He doubted very much if he could get any kind of extension from Garson. "How badly do you want to save the ranch?"

She blinked in surprise. "It's my home and Brandon's home. I don't have a problem selling off some of the land if I could keep the house."

Cade nodded. "Let me run through some ideas and see what I can do."

Brandon rushed into the room. "Cade, you ready to take me riding?"

Cade looked at Abby. "Well, that's up to your mother."

"You're probably tired. Maybe another time."

Brandon's chin nearly sagged to the floor. Cade

couldn't stand to disappoint him. "You know, I have some time. Maybe we can take a short ride."

Abby followed them outside. "Cade, you don't have to do this. I'll take him tomorrow."

"You know, I haven't done much riding since I've been home. I've kind of missed it. If I remember, your daddy had some good-looking horseflesh around here. Wouldn't mind getting a look at his mount."

"You mean Midnight Dancer," Brandon said. "Nobody has ridden him since Grandpa."

They went to the barn. Once inside, they walked down the center aisle, where Cade found several horses. But when they came to big box stall, he knew which horse was inside. The plaque on the door confirmed it—Midnight Dancer.

"Hi, boy," Brandon said as he approached the half door of the stall. The coal-black stallion immediately shied away and whinnied, then tossed his head and pranced around the stall. "Isn't he beautiful?"

"He sure is," Cade answered, then looked at Abby. "He's probably worth a lot. Have you thought about selling him?"

"I didn't want to rush into anything." She glanced at her son. "Dancer is Brandon's horse."

Cade nodded, and decided he would talk with Chance. His brother was the horse expert. They continued down the row and met up with Charlie. The foreman had saddled up two mounts. Cade watched Brandon. The seven-year-old apparently knew about horses, thanks to Tom Moreau. The boy easily climbed on a gentle gray mare, and Cade was given a roan. With a wave to Abby, they started out to the pasture. Not long past the gate, Brandon struck up a conversation.

"Do you ever miss your dad?"

Cade didn't know what to say. He had tried not to think about Jack Randell. The man had caused so much pain in his childhood. "I miss not having a dad, but I didn't like that he did something bad. But I was lucky to have Hank."

Brandon's small hands clutched the reins. "I don't miss my dad. I'm glad he and my mom aren't married anymore. He was mean to her."

Cade could hear the catch in the boy's voice. His grip on the reins tightened. "Did your dad ever hurt you?" he asked, not sure he wanted to hear the answer.

Brandon shook his head. "He tried one time, but Mom stopped him. After that we came to live with Grandpa."

"What about now? When you see your dad, how is he?"

"My dad never wants to see me. He hates me."

Abby knew her time was running out. Soon Cade would know about Brandon. Someone would see the resemblance. She'd caught Charlie watching the two together. He already knew because of his wife, Carmen.

Oh, God! She should have told him years ago. But after she'd married Joel, she didn't have that option. Now, how was she going to explain nearly eight years of silence? Cade would never understand. He'd never forgive her, either. She didn't care about that, though. Her only concern was what was best for her son. She had to tell Cade, but when?

The back door opened, and at the sound of her son's laughter Abby's chest tightened. How long had it been since he'd been happy? Tears filled her eyes, and she managed to blink them away by the time Brandon and Cade entered the kitchen.

"Oh, Mom, it was great." Brandon hugged her. "Thanks for letting Cade take me."

She smiled, trying to mask her uneasiness. "Well, I'm glad you had a good time." She looked at Cade. He, too, was smiling. "You look like you survived the ride."

"I got a few sore spots that will probably hurt more by tomorrow."

"Mom, Cade's a good rider, just like Grandpa."

"Well, honey, Cade grew up on a ranch. He even competed in some rodeos."

Brandon looked up at Cade, his dark eyes wide. "You did? Wow! Can you teach me to ride and rope?"

Abby and Cade both found themselves laughing.

"Whoa, son," Cade said, and Abby's heart skipped a beat. "I might be able to teach you a little roping for now, but broncos and bulls are out."

"But not right now," Abby said. "Why don't you go up and have your bath before supper, Brandon."

"Okay." Her son started to walk away, then stopped. "Can Cade eat with us?"

Abby drew a breath. This was her chance. "Why don't you ask him?"

"Please stay, Cade," Brandon begged. "Carmen made tamales."

"Wow, that's tough to turn down," Cade said as his gaze met hers. "If you're sure it's okay."

No, I'm not sure about anything, she cried silently, then swallowed her fear and answered, "It's fine. Besides, I need to talk to you about something…later."

Cade didn't know what to think about Abby's quick turnaround. "I guess I can stay."

"Yippee!" Brandon cried as he ran from the room. They were able to hear him all the way upstairs.

"Like I said before, that boy has too much energy."

Abby walked out of the kitchen and into the large living room. Cade followed, curious to know what she wanted.

"What do you want to talk about?"

"It's personal. If you don't mind, I'd rather wait until Brandon goes to bed."

He shrugged. "I can wait."

"Were you serious about my selling Dancer?" Abby asked as she sat down on the leather sofa.

Cade took the chair by the fireplace. "I'm sure he'd bring top dollar."

"What about using him for stud services?"

"I'm not an expert," he said. "I could ask Chance—"

Suddenly there was a crash upstairs and then a child's cry. "Oh, God." Abby took off up the steps, Cade right behind her.

In the bathroom, a naked Brandon lay facedown on the titled floor.

"Oh, Brandon, you're hurt." Abby knelt down beside him.

The boy raised his head, tears glistening in his eyes. "I slipped when I got out to get my GI Joe. I bumped my head."

"Here, let me check you out," Cade said, and crouched down on the boy's other side. He examined the child's limbs, then his neck to make sure there weren't any other injuries.

His gaze wandered over his back and stopped at the

sight of the half-moon-shaped birthmark at the base of his spine. Surprisingly it looked very similar to the ones his dad and brother Travis had.

A strange feeling came over Cade as he looked at Abby. Her worried expression was not just for her son's condition. The sudden jolt of awareness constricted his breathing. Now he knew why she'd been trying so hard to keep the boy away from him.

Brandon was his son.

Chapter Four

Brandon was his son.

Cade paced Tom Moreau's study. He was trying to control his emotions. The shock, anger and then the rush of unbelievable wonder.

He had a son.

Another rush of anger. How could Abby have kept Brandon from him all these years? Almost eight years. All this time Joel Garson got to play father. Fury ripped through him, restricting his ability to breathe, when he thought about how close Garson had come to abusing his child.

His son.

Cade was bombarded with strange new feelings—pride, protectiveness. A lump swelled in his throat as he thought about the little boy's dark eyes, the shy smile that revealed a missing tooth. The scattering of freckles along his nose that reminded him so much of Travis. A sudden tightness surrounded his heart. He wanted to run out and shout the news to the world.

He had a son.

And by God, he was going to be a part of his life.

Abby took longer than usual with Brandon, putting ice on his bump. She brought his dinner up on a tray, then sat with him while he ate. Cade hadn't stayed in the room. He told Brandon he would be back tomorrow. She had no doubt Cade would keep his word.

Abby remained in the sanctuary of Brandon's room until he was ready for bed. She assumed Cade was waiting for her downstairs. How was she going to explain the reason she'd kept his child from him?

Forty minutes later she entered the study to find Cade standing at the patio doors. He turned around to face her. If she hadn't known he hated her before, she knew it now. And she couldn't blame him.

"Why?" was all he said.

She drew a deep breath, trying to calm her trembling. "At the time I thought I was doing the right thing."

"What's right about keeping me from my son? For God's sake, Abby, I'm not a serial killer."

His eyes flashed with such rage she had to look away. "You didn't want me," she said.

"You're kidding, right?" he asked, his voice incredulous. "I asked you to marry me. I gave you a ring. I wanted you to go with me to Chicago."

She remained silent for a heartbeat, then said, "And when I called you a month later to tell you I was…pregnant, you didn't want to talk to me. And then when you finally came on the line, you told me it was good that we broke up. We were both too young to marry."

"Not once did you say you were carrying my child."

Abby wished she could make the pain in his eyes go away. "Okay, I was frightened, Cade. And young. Too young to—"

"To marry a Randell," he finished. "You didn't have any trouble walking down the aisle with Garson."

"What do you want me to say?" she pleaded. "That I handled it wrong?"

"You handled it the only way I expected you to. You went for the man with the name and the money." He glared at her. "Too bad it all backfired on you."

Abby ached to tell Cade what really happened, that her daddy made her send him away and pushed her to marry Joel. But she knew Cade was too angry to listen. He probably wouldn't believe her, anyway.

"That's right, it backfired," she said, knowing from the start her loveless marriage had been a mistake. "And I've been paying for my mistakes every day for nearly eight years."

"Well, my son isn't going to pay anymore," he said, his voice shaky. "We're not finished here, Abby. I'll be back. Tomorrow." He stormed out. Seconds later she heard the front door slam.

Abby sank onto the sofa as the tears she'd been holding back streamed down her face. She'd done everything all wrong. And Brandon had been the one who paid, and dearly. He'd been cheated of the father he deserved. More tears escaped, but Abby knew they would never cleanse her of what she'd done.

She'd already lost Cade. Now she could lose her son.

* * *

Abby was up early. Not that she'd gotten any sleep in the ten hours since Cade had left. But this morning she needed her strength. She knew that Cade would be back, demanding the right to see his son. But what rights did a part-time father have? He would go back to Chicago, and Abby would be a single parent again. The one thing she needed to do was protect Brandon, at least until she and Cade worked this out.

The doorbell rang, and Abby told Carmen that she would get it. She pulled open the door. Cade was dressed in a deep-blue polo shirt, jeans and boots. He held his hat in his hand.

"We need to talk," he announced as he stepped inside. He looked around. "Where's Brandon?"

"He's not here."

Cade's dark gaze swept her face. "What do you mean, he's not here? You knew I was coming by."

"And that's exactly why I sent him to day camp. I don't want him to overhear us arguing. He's spent most of his life in the middle of a turbulent relationship."

"Who's fault was that?"

His remark stung. "Look, if you can't be reasonable, we can hire a lawyer," Abby said, praying he wouldn't push for that.

He looked almost remorseful. "No. The last thing I want to do is bring in lawyers."

"Then stop the nasty remarks and let's see if we can work this out. We both want the same thing, what's best for Brandon."

Cade nodded, and Abby escorted him into the study and closed the door.

"I don't want you to tell Brandon you're his father,

not yet." She needed to establish that she had control of the situation.

Cade glared at her. "Like hell. I have rights."

"I didn't say I never want Brandon to know you're his father. I just don't want you to blurt it out right away. I need time."

"I'll agree to that if you promise to stay clear of Garson. I'm Brandon's father. I'll take care of him financially."

Joel had told her long ago that he would not pay for the child. "I only get alimony from Joel."

"Does he know that Brandon isn't his?"

"Yes, I told him. At first he said it didn't matter, but when Brandon was born...and when he began to look...more and more like you—" Abby paused "—Joel resented him."

"Is that when he started hitting you?"

She looked away, and Cade cursed.

Abby fought the flood of painful memories. She looked away, and Cade cursed.

"I don't want you anywhere near Garson again." He came up to her, and his hands gripped her arms. "I'll take care of you both."

Abby started to argue, but suddenly the fight left her and she nodded. "You take care of Brandon, but I don't want your money."

He glanced around. "By the looks of things, you don't have any choice."

Abby had learned one thing through therapy. She had choices. She pulled away from his touch. "I could sell the ranch and move into town," she said. "Then I won't need your money."

Cade wanted to laugh. For years he'd been envious of the Moreaus' and Garsons' money. It was ironic how the tables had turned. No matter how Abby hurt him by keeping his child from him, she was Brandon's mother. They needed to present a united front. And right now the ranch was in sorry shape. Something needed to be done immediately.

"Stuff your pride, Abigail. You *do* need my help. Because the bank is going to take this place away from you."

"The ranch is Brandon's. Dad left it to him. I'm the trustee until he's twenty-five."

"Great." Cade ran his fingers through his hair. How could he let Garson take away his son's legacy? "Then you had better hire me, and together we might just come up with a way to save at least part of this place."

"I can't afford to pay you," Abby said.

He knew that—he'd seen the books. "Don't worry, my fee is taken out of the profits, something you don't have to worry about right now."

Anger flared in her eyes. "You're really enjoying this, aren't you. Seeing a Moreau go under."

"If that's what I wanted, I wouldn't offer to help." Damn, why did she still get to him?

She stood there in her snug-fitting jeans. Her slim figure had filled out since she'd had Brandon. His gaze raised to meet hers. Underneath her fierce temper, he caught a glimpse of her vulnerability, and his chest tightened. She was in over her head. For that matter, so was he.

"Just remember, I'm doing this for Brandon, and only Brandon," he said.

"And that's the only reason I'm allowing you to help."

Cade nodded. "I'm going to need your power of attorney."

"Why?"

"So I can deal with the bank. I doubt you want to meet with your ex-husband again."

Cade went to the desk and pulled out the ledger he'd worked on the previous day. He sat down in the chair as if he belonged there. Abby couldn't help but wonder how things would have been different if she had told him about the baby when she called him in Chicago. Would they be married today? She quickly shook away the thought. It was too late. His hatred was enough to last a lifetime. Now she had to help him salvage a relationship with his son. At least until he returned to his life in Chicago.

"When are you going back to Chicago?"

Cade didn't look up from his work. "Not for a while. I've taken some leave from my job." He finally forced her. "I'm not going away, Abby. And nothing you say will make me leave my son."

That afternoon Cade went out to greet Chance, and together they walked to the Moreau barn.

"Thanks for coming by," Cade said.

"You said you needed a favor."

"Yeah. It looks like I'll be staying around awhile longer. I'm going to help Abby with the ranch. Seems she's in a financial bind."

A grin split his brother's face. "No need to explain any further. I understand."

"It's not what you think," Cade said. "This has nothing to do with Abby. It has to do with Brandon." Cade found he was shy about telling Chance. "Brandon...is my son."

Chance's mouth fell open. "Well, I'll be damned," he breathed. "When...how...? You just find out?"

"Yeah. Not that Abby was willing to tell me anything. I found a half-moon birthmark on Brandon's back. Abby couldn't deny it."

"Damn! She kept it from you all this time."

"Yeah, she married Garson after I went to Chicago." Cade couldn't keep the bitterness out of his voice. "She said she called me but couldn't tell me about the baby."

Chance slapped him on the back. "Well, congratulations, Dad. How does Brandon feel about this?"

"We decided to wait a while to tell him."

"Probably wise. Any chance you and Abby will get together and be a family?"

Cade shook his head. "She kept this from me, Chance. I don't think I can ever trust her."

"She must think she had her reasons. You know a lot of marriages have started out with less." His brother grinned. "All Joy and I had was a contract, no more than a business deal. And look what happened."

Cade didn't believe in miracles. He and Abby were history. "All I'm worried about is being a good father to Brandon."

"You and the boy are getting along, aren't you?"

Cade shrugged. "I guess, but I'm flying blind. You got any pointers?"

"Just love him."

Cade felt emotions churning inside him. "That's the easy part. He's a great kid. And he's been through so much. He loves the ranch. But if I don't do something fast, he's going to lose it."

"What can I do to help?" Chance asked.

"I was hoping you'd ask. Think you could handle another stud in your stable for a while?"

"What stud?"

"Midnight Dancer?"

Chance's eyes rounded. "Are you kidding? That horse has an impeccable bloodline."

"Do you think you could spread the word that he's available?"

"No problem. Why don't you and Abby come over to the house tonight? We can talk about this some more."

"No need. I'm handling the Moreau ranch business now. You can deal with me."

Chance raised an eyebrow. "Wouldn't it just be considerate to include Abby?"

At the moment Cade didn't want to be anywhere near Abby. His anger was still so out of control he was afraid he'd say something he'd regret. But the truth was they had a son together, and he would have to spend some time with her. "Okay, I'll bring her along, but warn Joy not to try anything."

Chance didn't hide his grin. "I have no idea what you're talking about."

"Oh, God, save me from people in love." Cade turned and stalked off. It was envy, pure and simple. He wanted what his brother had, but a long time ago Abby had made sure he would never have it.

Abby pulled into the driveway about eight-thirty that evening. She shut off the engine and fluffed her hair to make sure she was presentable. She was crazy to even care. Cade hated her so much he could hardly stand to be around her. He wouldn't notice she was wearing a royal-blue blouse. His favorite color. He'd said blue turned her eyes aquamarine. A thrill rushed through her body as she remembered how Cade had always made her feel beautiful.

But that had been so long ago. Joel's cruelty had almost washed away those sweet memories. Nothing had ever pleased her husband. She had never looked good enough, could never dress elegantly enough for the wife of a bank executive. Abby winced, still able to feel the blows as Joel struck her once, twice. A whimper escaped her, then a cry. She didn't even notice the tears until she heard her name.

"Abby…"

She jerked her head toward the window and found Cade. He was leaning against her car, looking confused. "Cade, you startled me." She glanced away and quickly wiped her eyes.

"Are you okay?" His voice held concern, but she knew better.

"I'm fine. Just tired." Masking her emotions, she opened the door and climbed out of the car. "I'd like to get this over with quickly." She didn't want to be with Cade any more than he wanted to be with her.

"Okay, let's go." Cade took her elbow and led her up to the porch, where they were met at the door by Chance and his wife.

"Welcome," Joy said with a warm smile.

Chance pushed open the screen door, and they walked into the large entry with its polished hardwood floor covered partly with an area rug. At the end of the entry was a staircase with newel posts and wheat-colored carpeting.

"Why don't we go into the dining room?" Joy suggested. "It's about the only place in the house that isn't torn apart from the remodeling."

Abby went with Joy, and the two brothers followed. The large room was papered in a rose-and-green print, and the long mahogany table was surrounded by six high-back chairs.

"It's beautiful," Abby said, knowing that every piece of furniture was most likely an antique.

"Thanks, but I had nothing to do with this. My aunt Lillian left me the house and all the furnishings. Chance and I just cleaned and polished a little to find the beauty underneath."

"Chance, you wanted to discuss Midnight Dancer," Cade said, pulling them right to the reason for their visit.

With a frown at his brother, Chance went to the head of the table. The brothers resembled each other, but Chance's hair was lighter. "Please sit down, Abby," he invited. "Cade mentioned you were thinking about putting the stallion out to stud?"

Everyone sat, and Abby shot a quick glance at Cade. "He thinks it can make some money for the ranch." She was finished being embarrassed. "And as you must know, I can use some fast cash."

"Ranching is a tough business," Chance said. "We all run into problems. So if we can help…" He smiled and looked at his wife. The love between them was evident with every glance.

"I appreciate that. But right now I'd be happy if you could help me with Midnight Dancer."

"That's all I wanted to hear," Chance said. "I made some calls today and already have two people interested." He opened a file on the table and handed her what appeared to be a contract. "I don't usually board studs, preferring to keep to my own stock, but

I'll take Dancer and handle his breeding for a percentage of the fee.''

Abby glanced down at the enormous stud fee and stopped breathing. "You can get this much?"

Chance nodded. "If you sign the contract, I'll have the mares here as soon as they're ready."

Abby handed Cade the contract. "What do you think?"

"It's a fair deal," he agreed. "And it's fast cash, which is the important thing. How do you think Brandon will feel about this?"

Abby was touched that he asked about her son—correction, their son. "I don't know. This is a lot better than having to sell Dancer."

Chance spoke up. "If it ever comes to that, I'd like to have first chance to buy him. He's a magnificent animal."

"It won't come to that," Cade said. "Dancer is Brandon's, and I'll make sure that never changes."

Abby was quickly becoming angry. Cade might have rights, but she didn't like him forcing his way into their lives. She turned back to Chance. "Okay, I'll do it." She took the pen and signed.

Just then a baby's soft cries came from the monitor on the table. "Looks like our daughter needs some attention." Joy stood and started to leave, then turned to Abby. "Would you like to see Katie?"

"I'd love to," Abby said, and followed Joy out of the room.

Cade watched the two go, unable to read Abby's thoughts. Did she understand they had a lot more work to do to save the ranch? This was a good start. He turned back to his brother. "I can't thank you enough for doing this."

Chance shrugged. "No problem. In fact, I should be thanking you. This might be a new business venture for me." His eyebrows drew together. "What about you, bro? How are you doing?"

Cade stood. "I don't know. I'm still trying to get used to the idea of being a father. It's like I've been sucker-punched in the gut."

"I know. None of this can be easy. Just remember Brandon needs you. He's pretty much been left out in the cold in the father department. I know Tom Moreau was around, but he's gone now." A smiled appeared on Chance's face. "And that kid is real taken with you. Just a little suggestion. Be careful how you act around Abby. She is Brandon's mother, and he's very protective of her. Must be the Randell in him. And you know how we've always watched out for each other."

Brandon Randell, Cade thought. "When all this is straightened out, I want my son to have our name. Of course, I don't know if that would be a good idea. Some people still connect our name to trouble."

"I used to think that, too," Chance said. "But there's another generation of Randells now. Brandon and Katie. We have to be the ones to teach them to be proud of where they came from. Now come on, smile. You have a son."

Cade felt his emotions surface. He was proud of that little guy. "You're right."

"Damn straight I am. He's a good-looking boy, but not as cute as my princess. Come on, let's go see her."

They climbed the stairs and walked down the hall to the nursery. Inside they found the ladies, but it wasn't Joy holding the baby. Abby sat in the rocking chair with little Katie snuggled against her breast.

A fierce pain shot through Cade's heart as he thought about all the years he'd missed with his son. He'd never gotten to see his son suckle at his mother's breast or watch him take his first steps or hear him say his first word.

And it hurt. More than he'd ever imagined it could.

Cade was exhausted, but he kept the cows moving. The past two days he'd spent working with Chance at his ranch, and then in the evenings he went to the Moreau ranch. He had told Abby straight out that he wanted time with his son, and she had agreed. She even gave the two of them time alone to get to know each other.

Chance rode up next to him. "When are you going back to Chicago?"

Cade tugged the reins and slowed his mount, careful to stay with the group of stray cows. "Trying to get rid of me? But hey, if you don't need me, I can go help Hank."

"I didn't say that, Bro, but this can't be much of a vacation for you."

"I'm not on vacation any longer."

"And you're not a rancher, either." Chance pushed back his hat and squinted at the hot sun. "Don't you want to spend this time with Brandon?"

"Brandon is at day camp. I'll see him tonight when he gets home."

"How have things been between you and Abby?"

"There's nothing between me and Abby and never will be. Outside of business we have nothing to talk about."

"Sure," Chance said. "I'd say you're running

scared. You've also been itching for a fight ever since you first saw Abby at the party.''

"What the hell are you talking about?''

"She still gets to you, doesn't she? That's the reason you can't face being alone with her.''

"I'd say I have plenty of reasons not to want to see Abby. For one, she kept my son from me. And if I hadn't found out about Brandon myself, she'd still be keeping him a secret.''

"I'm not saying what Abby did was right,'' Chance said, "but because you two share a son, you have to find a way to get past the anger.''

Cade stared at the open plains, listened to the cattle bawling as they wandered toward the pasture. He was hot, sweaty and smelled of cows. And he realized he'd missed it. The land had been hard to work, but there was satisfaction in completing the task. Most of all, he wanted to be around to see Brandon grow up. He knew too well what it was like without a dad. But seeing Abby... "I don't know if I can.''

Chance leaned a gloved hand on his saddle horn. "Give yourself some time. This father stuff is new. Is there anything I can do to help?''

"Oh, yeah, you have so much experience,'' Cade teased. "How old is Katie—two months?''

"Close to, and she adores me,'' Chance bragged.

"All I know is that your wife and child sure have sweetened your disposition.''

Chance grinned. "You should try it.''

"You want me to start something up with Abby?''

"Like you haven't had the hots for her since tenth grade.''

"I'm not an oversexed teenager any longer.'' But Cade knew that Abby Garson could tempt a saint.

"Then concentrate on a relationship with your son."

"That's all I want," Cade said, trying to convince himself as much as his brother.

Chapter Five

A few days later Cade glanced around the Circle B's kitchen table. Hank and Ella were there, as well as Joy and Chance. Cade had already told everyone about Brandon being his son but made them promise to keep the news to themselves for a while.

"I called the family together because I need your help."

Hank smiled. "If this is about Brandon, we already consider him family."

"Thanks, Hank," Cade said. "That means a lot to me."

"Well, he's a sweet boy," the housekeeper added. "I'm going to plan a big party to welcome him to the family."

Cade raised his hand. "Hold that thought, Ella." He smiled at the housekeeper. "But you'll be the first to know when the time comes. Right now, there are other things I need to deal with. The Moreau ranch. Seems Tom left a hefty debt for Abby." He glanced around the room, not seeing any surprised looks. "I've been going over the books, trying to find something that will give Abby some fast cash. Selling her herd seems to be the best way to do that. So we need to have a roundup."

"How soon do you want us?" Chance asked.

Cade wasn't surprised by his brother's response. "As soon as possible. I was thinking this weekend, if that's not too-short notice."

Hank leaned back in his chair. "Son, I'm willing to help out, but selling a few head of cattle won't take care of Tom's debt."

"I know, Hank. I've also listed some Moreau real estate, hoping it'll sell fast." Cade sighed, knowing this was all an uphill battle. "My big concern is Garson and the bank note. I doubt he's going to be real helpful to his ex-wife."

Hank shook his head. "Tom sure left that gal with a mess. Is Abby going to try and rebuild the ranch?"

Cade shrugged. "It's possible, if done right. But it's going to take a long time. That's why I wanted to toss out an idea I've been mulling over. I've read about ranchers who turn part of their land into nature retreats."

Cade received only blank stares as responses but continued, "Around here, there's enough wildlife to make an attractive vacation spot. A lot of people want time away from the city and their busy lives. They want to come to a quiet place. I was thinking about using the part of the Moreau ranch that borders Mustang Valley."

Cade swallowed hard, hoping he wasn't overstepping his bounds when he asked, "Hank, I was wondering if you'd be interested in going along with this.

It could be a good business venture. Your strip of property along the other side of the creek would be perfect," he said, then hurried on. "The only changes we'd make to the land would be hiking trails and some guest cabins. And I'll front the money to have them built. Mustang Valley could be a great draw."

Hank frowned. "Wouldn't that bring a lot of traffic and people into that area?"

"Not if we don't want. We'll protect the land. Take our time. We can do as much or as little as we want. A few cabins, add more later if this works. We won't allow cars in the area, only horses and bicycles and hikers—people these days are into walking. Nature lovers and birders would have a heyday in the valley. Believe me, this could be a money-maker." He looked at Joy and Chance. "Your ranch is just beyond the valley, but we could include the strip along the small lake. Then we can offer swimming and fishing. And so it doesn't interfere with our family's privacy, you can reserve a month where we have the area to ourselves."

Joy's blue eyes sparkled as she looked at Chance. "I would like to see some improvements at the lake so we could take Katie there when she's older." She turned back to Cade. "How does Abby feel about this?"

"I haven't approached her with the idea yet because I wanted you all to have a chance to think about it first. I know what the valley means to all of us, and I'd never do anything to jeopardize that."

Finally Chance spoke up, "So you think a...nature retreat can generate enough income to save the Moreau ranch?"

"Not by itself," Cade said. "Abby will have to

lease out some of her grazing land for a while. I'm also going to talk to her about eventually expanding the entire operation into a working guest ranch.''

"Unbelievable," Hank said, shaking his head. "You think city people will pay to work on a ranch?"

Cade nodded. "Yeah, I do. In Chicago, my co-workers thought my life in the 'Wild West' was a lot more interesting than working in an office." He grinned. "With the help of the Internet, we can advertise all over the country. The world, even."

Hank didn't say anything for a long time, then he finally stood. "Since my birthday, I've been doing a lot of thinking. I'd planned to wait until Travis made it home again, but I guess this is as good a time as any." He drew a breath, and Cade stole a glance at his brother, seeing worry mirrored on his face.

"I'm getting too old to handle the ranch on my own." His soft hazel eyes met Cade and Chance. "You boys have been my only family—like my own sons. So I decided to sign over the Circle B to you three. You all can decide about this nature-retreat stuff."

Cade swallowed. "Hank, I never expected... I never meant for you to give away the land."

Hank grinned. "If it'll bring all you boys home, I'll wish I'd done it years ago. I think I may just enjoy being retired. Gives me time to spoil the grandkids." He turned and walked out of the room.

The room was silent after Hank's news. Cade glanced at Chance. His older brother looked just as confused as he felt. "I guess," Chance said, "we should call Travis and see how he feels about this."

Yeah, Cade would like to talk to Travis again. Since his younger brother had left town, Cade had only been able to reach his answering machine, and Travis hadn't returned his calls. Maybe Chance would have better luck.

"Yeah, you do that," Cade said. "And I better go see Abby." A sudden excitement raced through him. He was home, and this time he was staying. He was going to build a life for himself and his son. He only hoped Abby would feel the same way about him hanging around.

That evening after their ride, Brandon was brushing down Smoky in her stall while Cade put away the tack. He had brought the bay gelding, Gus, over from the Circle B, deciding it was more convenient to board his horse here.

"When do you have to go back to Chicago?" Brandon asked as Cade was coming out of the tack room.

Cade went into the stall. "I guess I didn't tell you, but I'll be hanging around for a while."

The boy didn't show any emotion. "Why?"

"Because I'm trying to help your mom with the ranch."

"But that's Charlie's job."

"I'm not trying to take Charlie's job. I'm helping with the financial part. So the ranch will still be making money by the time you're old enough to run it. You can say I'm looking after your interests."

The boy smiled and Cade felt his heart lurch in his chest. "You mean you work for me? I'm the boss?" Brandon said.

"You think you're a hotshot, don't you, kid?" Cade reached for the boy and began to tickle him, then tossed him over his shoulder, enjoying the sweet sound of his giggles.

Once Brandon was back on his feet, he looked up at Cade. "I'm glad you're staying. It's like…it's like having…"

"What?" Cade asked.

"It's like having a dad," Brandon said. Then before Cade could react, the boy picked up the brush and began to work on his mare again.

Cade just stood there, trying to regain his composure, aching to claim his son. He swallowed and managed to say, "I'm glad I can be here for you."

Abby walked into the barn and watched for a few moments. She had to admit she was a little jealous of the budding relationship between Cade and Brandon. They had grown so close in just a few short weeks. And soon he would know Cade was his real father. Would her son hate her?

Brandon suddenly spotted her. "Hi, Mom. Cade and I rode over to the lake by Chance and Joy's house. We got to see Katie, too. Joy even let me hold her."

"Is that so? She's pretty cute, huh?"

Brandon nodded. "She grabbed my finger."

"Sounds like you had a busy afternoon."

He smiled. "It was fun."

She glanced at her watch. "And you have a busy day tomorrow, too. How about a bath, then to bed?"

Brandon started to argue, then looked at Cade. "Okay, Mom. I'll just put the brush away." He hurried off to the tack room.

Abby turned to Cade. "Please, tell me what you did to Brandon so he didn't argue."

Cade shrugged. "Not much. I just told him that moms are special, and we shouldn't give them a hard time."

Her chest tightened. Maybe Cade didn't hate her. "Thank you."

"No problem." He gave the horse one last pat, then walked out of the stall and shut the gate. He stood beside her, his dark eyes locked with hers. A warmth spread through her. "Abby, do you think we can talk after Brandon goes to bed?" he asked.

She didn't like the sound of this. "Sure."

Brandon returned and all three of them walked to the house. For a split second, Abby pretended they were a family.

An hour later Abby sat and listened silently as Cade explained plans for the nature retreat. Cade found he really wanted her approval, not just her willingness to go along with the idea.

Silently she got up and walked across the room to the doors to the patio and looked out. "You know, never once did my dad or my husband ask me how I felt about anything. My dad didn't even leave me the ranch. He was upset because I divorced Joel." She looked at Cade, who'd stood up, too, and her eyes were like sparkling emeralds. "Thank you, Cade. Thank you for caring about my feelings."

Cade cursed Moreau silently. "You control the ranch, Abby. The final decision is yours."

She shook her head. "You could have said it was the only way to make a go of the ranch."

"I'm still not sure if it's the solution to your problems," he told her honestly.

"I owe you a lot just for trying."

Cade watched her. Abby wore her usual outfit of jeans and boots, but the rich-blue blouse she wore did unbelievable things to her eyes and skin. When she finally turned, a shy smiled teased her lips, and his pulse went into overdrive.

He wanted to hate her, but he couldn't. The young Abby he'd known had loved her father, had always ached for his approval. Obviously Moreau hadn't wanted his only daughter hooking up with a Randell. So instead, he'd pushed her into an abusive marriage.

"Was your marriage to Garson ever happy?" The question surprised Cade just as much as it did Abby. But he had to make sense of why she'd wanted Joel over him.

She shook her head.

He stepped toward her. "When did he start beating you?"

Her gaze darted away. "Joel didn't always hit me. I think he was as surprised as I was when it first happened."

"When did it happen?"

She shrugged.

"Tell me, Abby. I need to know." He was beside her now.

"It was at Brandon's fourth birthday. There were a lot of kids and their parents at the party. One of the fathers remarked about Brandon's coloring. Why was he so dark when both Joel and I were fair? After everyone left, Joel had a few drinks. Then he tried to pick a fight, which ended when he struck me with his fist."

Cade watched a tear slide down her cheek. Unable to resist he reached out and drew her into his arms. She was so soft it was incredible. "But he knew that Brandon wasn't his."

Abby nodded against his chest. "When Joel proposed, I told him no. But he was persistent, so I blurted out that I was pregnant. He said it didn't matter. He would be the baby's father. Even when Brandon was born seven and a half months later, no one questioned it. As Brandon got older, he began to look like you. Then when someone else noticed the difference, he went crazy.''

''So he decided to take it out on you—to beat you.'' Her sobs increased, and he continued to hold her. ''The man's a bastard,'' he growled.

''Please, I don't want to talk about Joel,'' Abby pleaded.

She raised her head, her eyes glistening with tears. Cade's body stirred, and the last thing on his mind was comforting her. He lowered his mouth to hers.

The taste of Cade's mouth was like an awakening to Abby, and she opened to him eagerly, seeking his warmth and touch. It had been so long, so long since anyone had held her. She reveled in the familiarity of his hard body and wrapped her arms around his neck. She felt Cade's shudder and clung to him as his tongue pushed inside her mouth, teasing and stroking. Then all too soon, he broke off the kiss and released her so suddenly she stumbled backward.

''Cade,'' she whispered, but he only turned away.

Abby stared at his broad back and saw he was having trouble regaining his composure.

''That shouldn't have happened,'' he finally said. ''I'm here for Brandon. Not to relive my randy youth.''

His words stung. ''I didn't kiss you—*you* kissed me,'' she snapped.

He swung around, his eyes dark with anger. ''There's never been any doubt that I wanted you, Abby,'' he said, his gaze hot. ''Now that I satisfied my curiosity, we can get on with business. Do you want me to get started on the plans for the retreat?''

Trying to keep her own composure, she nodded. "Whatever you think is best."

"It's not a good idea to be too trusting," he warned.

"I'm not worried. I have nothing to lose anymore. Besides, you're Brandon's father. I know you have his best interests at heart."

"Just remember he's the *only* reason I'm here." He glared at her, then turned and stormed out.

Abby had thought she was used to his rejection, but as the door slammed behind him, she realized she wasn't. It still stung. But like other things she'd had to deal with, somehow she would get through this. Somehow she'd get past the fury she saw in Cade's eyes and the fear that she might lose Brandon, simply because she wanted her son to know his father.

A few days later Cade entered the bank, hating that he had to swallow his pride and ask Garson for a favor. But he didn't have much choice. There were only ten days left until the loan was due and she wouldn't take a loan from him. Maybe Joel Garson would feel generous and agree to give Abby an extension for another three months. Cade doubted it. So until he was able to sell the lakefront property, he'd have to get more capital together.

His thoughts went to Abby. He never should have kissed her. He was driving himself crazy. Why couldn't he just stop his thoughts of her? She was nothing to him. Abby Moreau didn't want him years ago, and he didn't want her now. Warmth rushed through his body as he remembered how she felt in his arms, how sweet she tasted. Stop it, he told himself. He had to keep his relationship with Abby purely business, for his son.

Cade made his way to the executive offices. He looked through the glass-enclosed office to find, Joel seated at his desk. After drawing a deep breath, Cade knocked on the door. The man was expecting him, so there wasn't any reason to wait. Opening the door, he walked in. By the look on Garson's face, Cade knew he wasn't happy to see him, instead of Abby. Good.

"Garson. I think you know why I'm here," Cade announced as he set his briefcase on the edge of the desk and sat down across from the man. "The Moreau ranch."

Joel leaned back in his leather chair and smiled. "So you want a favor, Randell. How interesting. And just what am I going to get in return?"

Cade hated his smug look but ignored it. He pulled a paper out of his briefcase and shoved it across the desk. "You can add another quarter percent on the loan rate, and of course the late fees."

Joel went over the contract. "Quite impressive. Looks like your schooling paid off. I hear you've done pretty well for yourself in Chicago. So why are you hanging around here?"

"Look, Garson, let's not pretend we ever liked each other. Forget the small talk. I'm here for a business deal. And only that. If you're interested, let me know."

"Why should I do anything to help your bastard son?"

Cade clenched his fists but controlled the urge to smash Garson's smirking face. "Leave Brandon out of this."

Joel stood and came around the desk. "But isn't

this all to save his ranch?'' he asked as he perched his bulky body on the edge. "Why should I want to help...a Randell?''

Cade jumped up, grabbed Joel by the lapels of his expensive suit, then shoved him back against the wall. Cade could smell the alcohol as Garson gasped for air. "It isn't so much fun when you're on the receiving end, is it.''

Joel struggled. "Let go of me, Randell, or I'll call Security.''

"And I'll call the bank's corporate office and tell them that one of their managers reeks of bourbon at nine in the morning.''

"Go to hell.''

"Not before you.'' Cade released him. "I'm leaving now, but you say one thing about my son, and you'll be sorry.''

"Well, you can forget about any extension on the loan. I will personally foreclose on the ranch on the first of the month. Unless, of course, you can write out a check for the balance due.''

Cade smiled. "You might be surprised at what I can do. Don't worry, Garson, one way or the other, I'll have the money for you. And don't be surprised if Circle B pulls their account out of here. We don't do business with a man who has a drinking problem.''

Garson's face turned red with anger. "Get out. I'll make sure you can't get a loan anywhere in this town.''

"As if I need your help.'' Cade picked up his briefcase and walked out, knowing he could easily pay off the Moreau ranch's debts. But he knew Abby had too much pride to take anything from him.

In the parking lot Cade climbed into the ranch truck

he'd been driving since his return home. He picked up the cell phone from the seat and punched in the real-estate agent's number. He prayed Nancy Painter had had better luck than he had.

"Painter Realty," a woman answered.

"Hello, Nancy, it's Cade Randell. Please tell me you have some good news about the Moreau property."

"Oh, Cade, I was going to call you later."

"You have a buyer?"

"No, not exactly. We do have someone interested. Are you prepared to lower your asking price?"

He'd lowered it as far as he dared. The lakefront property was too valuable to just give away. "No, Nancy. That's as low as I can go."

"I understand, Cade." She sighed. "Please give me a little more time."

Cade knew that without selling the property, Abby couldn't pay the loan. Suddenly an idea came to him. If he kept it quiet, he could help out until another buyer was found. By then everything would be fine. And Abby would be safe from Garson. For good.

That weekend several trucks pulling horse trailers drove into the Moreau ranch. Neighbors showed up to help with the roundup. Hank, Ella, Chance and Joy, carrying Katie, all appeared at the house. Abby was overwhelmed by the support they were giving her.

"Hear you're having a roundup," Hank said.

"That's what I've been told." Abby stepped aside and allowed the group into the house. "I'm so glad you came."

Ella was carrying a large pot as she stepped through the door. "Just show Joy and me to the kitchen."

"And I'll go and get settled in the bunkhouse," Hank said.

"Oh, Hank, I have plenty of room for you all to stay in the house," Abby offered.

The old man smiled, and deep lines appeared at the corners of his eyes. "That's mighty neighborly, Abby, but I kind of like to hang around with the guys, playin' a little cards and catchin' up on local news."

Abby smiled. "I understand. Well, Charlie has everything ready, but I'll expect you here for supper."

"Wouldn't miss it." He hugged her. Touched by the man's open affection, Abby wondered why her dad couldn't have been more like Hank.

"Mom! Mom!" Brandon called as he hurried into the house. "Guess what? I'm going to sleep out in the bunkhouse with the guys."

"Oh, honey, maybe you should stay at the house. They're getting up pretty early."

"I know. So am I."

Abby sighed as Cade walked into the house. She looked at him pleadingly, hoping he'd tell their son he was too young to go on the roundup.

"Look, Brandon," Cade said as he crouched down to eye level with the boy. "I think all morning in the saddle is a bit much for you."

"But you said I was a good rider. I want to go." Tears formed in his eyes. "I'm not a baby."

"We know you're not a baby, but we have to move the herd tomorrow. It's not an easy job. You've never worked with a cow horse, and the roundup arrived before I got a chance to show you how. There's a Circle B roundup in the fall. I'll work to get you ready for that one. Promise."

The room grew silent as Brandon hung his head.

Abby's heart went out to Cade, knowing this was the hardest part of parenting. She could see how much he hated telling his son no.

"I have an idea," Cade began. "Tomorrow you can watch for us with binoculars, and when you see the dust from the herd, you can ride out and meet us."

The boy's eyes rounded. "Wow, you mean it?"

Cade glanced at Abby. "If it's okay with your mom."

There was no way she was going spoil her son's day. "I think you're old enough to do that."

Brandon hugged her. "Thanks, Mom." He turned back to Cade and threw his arms around him. "Thanks, Cade."

Abby didn't miss the emotion in Cade's eyes as his arms closed around his son. Finally he released him and stood. "Now, go get your things for the bunkhouse."

When Brandon ran upstairs, Cade spoke to Abby. "I'll make sure he's all right," he promised. "He'll be home by breakfast."

She nodded, grateful and surprised he was so considerate of her feelings. "That's fine. I'm sure Brandon will enjoy himself, and I can concentrate on cooking."

A smile broke out on Cade's face. "That's what I like to hear, ladies cooking. What's on the menu?"

"We're just going to surprise you," Ella said. "Now go do something with your horses so we can get our work done." She shooed Hank and Cade out of the house. The women went into the kitchen to find that Carmen had already made tamales for dinner, so they went to work on tomorrow's menu.

Abby was glad she had something to keep her busy.

She didn't want to think about how close Brandon and Cade were becoming. She had to get used to the fact that Cade was going to be a part of their lives. Brandon needed a father. Something she hadn't been able to give her son until now. And it looked as if Cade was serious about his role.

Late that evening Abby sat on the patio and watched the reflection of the moonlight in the pool. Many changes were happening, and fast. Tomorrow was going to be busy, but she was happy about that. For so many years she and Brandon had been isolated. Joel hadn't been much of a family man, and when he drank, she and her son stayed away. Now she had people around. This house had been like a tomb, and not just since her father's death, but long before that. Since her mother was alive.

Abby remembered being a five-year-old girl. All the parties at the Moreau ranch. How beautiful her mother looked and how much her father loved his wife. Had it been Jessica Moreau's untimely death that turned Tom into a bitter man and made him resent his only child?

Abby knew her childhood hadn't been a normal one. Her father never wanted to spend time with her. So the staff had become her family, starting with Carmen and Charlie. She played with the kids of the ranch workers. Then in high school, she met Cade. He had a bad reputation. At first she'd been shy and wondered why he wanted to spend time with her. She'd heard the other kids talk about his wild ways, about his ex-con father, but she didn't care. Cade was good to her. He cared about her. And she soon fell in love with him.

Abby closed her eyes and sighed. She hadn't meant to hurt him. But she'd had no choice. Her father had forced her. By the time she got the courage to tell Cade about the baby, it was too late to get him back. Now it was years too late.

A tear fell and Abby brushed it away. The only consolation was that she had his son. A part of Cade would always be with her.

"Abby…"

She recognized Cade's voice and quickly composed herself before turning around.

"Cade. What are you doing here?"

He was dressed in new-looking jeans and a white shirt. "I put some papers away in the study. What are you doing out here? Tomorrow's going to be a long day, and five o'clock comes around awfully early."

She nodded. "I know. I'm a rancher's daughter."

"I doubt you ever had to get out of bed at dawn to go round up cows."

Angry, Abby stood. "How do you know? You have no idea what it was like to live under Tom Moreau's roof." She marched across the patio to get away from the man who didn't miss an opportunity to try to get to her.

Cade knew he was always saying the wrong thing, pushing her buttons. Why couldn't he stop? He started after her, but hesitated a safe distance away. "Abby, I'm sorry. That was uncalled for."

She sighed and faced him. "Forget it. We're all under a lot of stress. I'm sorry I jumped on you."

Stress was an understatement, Cade thought as he watched the moonlight shine on her hair. She had on a blue cotton shirt tucked into a pair of tan shorts. Damn, she had good-looking legs. He quickly pulled his wayward attention back to her face, to find her eyes misty and wistful. He lowered his gaze to her mouth. A mouth he knew would feel silky and soft to the touch, a mouth that roused his hunger until he thought he'd go crazy.

Something inside him snapped, and he went to her, telling himself he was only going to hold her, comfort her. When he reached for her, she went willingly into his arms. He bit back a groan as she pressed her body to his. They fit perfectly. Too perfectly, and he wanted her. No matter how many years had passed, that had never changed.

He leaned back and saw the desire in her eyes. ''Abby,'' he breathed, unable to fight it any longer. His mouth lowered to hers.

A light flashed through the kitchen window and caught Cade's eye. When he heard voices, he jerked back. As his head cleared, he realized he'd almost made another big mistake. He couldn't let himself get involved with Abby again.

''I've got to go.'' He saw her hurt look but ignored it. If he didn't leave now, he didn't know if he could. ''I'll see you at breakfast.'' He started out to the yard, praying she wouldn't call him back because he knew he'd go to her.

Chapter Six

Not wanting to face Cade after last night, Abby managed to avoid him at breakfast. They'd been so close,
but in the end he'd rejected her again. She'd decided
to stay in the kitchen and help with the cooking while
Ella served the food in the bunkhouse. Finally the
dozen men rode out just as the sun was coming up.

But Abby knew it was only a short reprieve. They'd
be back by noon with the herd. And if somehow she
managed to get through this day without seeing Cade,
he would be around tomorrow, and the day after that.
And somehow she would have to live with the fact
that he couldn't stand being near her.

She buried her face in her hands. Was this some
kind of punishment for what she'd done? Hadn't she
paid enough?

"Abby, are you all right?"

Abby's head jerked up. Joy was standing a few feet
away, looking concerned. "I'm fine," she lied. "Just
tired."

Joy smiled. "I know, but roundups are fun, aren't they?"

She boosted little Katie higher in her arms. The Three-month-old was cute, with her blond hair spiked out around her chubby face.

"They're a lot of work," Abby countered.

Joy shrugged. "I guess I don't think about the work. I remember the Circle B's roundup. That's when Chance told me he realized he couldn't live without me."

Abby was confused. "But you were married before that, weren't you?"

Joy blushed and glanced at her daughter. "I'm the one who asked Chance to marry me—to help me keep Katie."

Abby shook her head. "I don't understand."

Joy sighed as she stroked her baby's head. "You see, my in-laws were trying to take my daughter. Chance agreed to the marriage, but only because I offered to sell him part of my ranch."

"Oh, my," Abby said as she sank into a kitchen chair. "I didn't know."

"It's not exactly something a woman wants broadcast to the world. It was a pretty rocky start, even more difficult when we had to act married for others." Another smile appeared on Joy's face. "The kissing, the touching and sharing a bedroom. Well, let me tell you…I was happy to see that Chance was getting antsy."

"How did you finally…get together?"

Joy blushed prettily. "That took a wicked thunderstorm and a lot of determination on my part." She tossed Abby a knowing look. "But I've found the Randell men are worth the effort."

Abby looked away. There was no way she and Cade would end up like Chance and Joy. "Not everyone felt that way about them." She remembered her father's hatred for the Randells.

"But you and I do. Aren't we lucky they were such a well-kept secret?" Joy grew serious. "I know you and Cade have a history...and a wonderful son. It would be great if you could somehow work things out...between you two."

Abby closed her eyes, wishing it was that easy. "It's too late. What was between Cade and me was a long time ago. And I destroyed any feelings he had for me when I sent him away." She shook her head. "The only thing Cade feels for me now is disgust."

"You have to give him time. The Randell brothers have carried a lot of baggage around for a lot of years. But like I said before, they are well worth it." She leaned forward. "If you ask me, Cade protests too much about you. That has me wondering who he's trying to convince."

Before Abby could say anything, Brandon came charging into the house. "Mom, I see 'em coming!" he hollered. "The dust from the cows. Cade even waved at me."

"Then I guess you better get going," she said as she followed her excited son outside to the barn. Brandon's horse was already saddled and waiting in the corral.

"Now don't get crazy and go tearing out there and scaring the cattle."

With a boost up from Abby, Brandon was seated in the saddle. "I won't, Mom. Bye." He used the reins to turn his horse, Smoky, toward the gate, where one of the ranch hands let him out.

Abby watched Brandon ride off. She told herself that she wanted to make sure he made it safely. She lifted the binoculars that were hanging on the post, then looked out to the rise and spotted a rider coming toward Brandon. Cade. When father and son met, Brandon smiled. Cade smiled, too, as he tugged at his son's hat playfully. Abby's stomach tightened with longing. She wanted to be with them. But she couldn't. She should get used to the two of them sharing things without her. A rush of sadness came over her as she watched the two ride off together. Nothing was ever going to be the same again.

Cade was dirty, thirsty and tired of hearing the sound of bawling cows by the time he rode back toward the holding pens outside the corral.

If the guys in Chicago could see him now, they wouldn't think being a cowboy was so glamorous. Well, he wasn't about to tell them any different. They could find out for themselves after they stayed a week at the Moreau Guest Ranch.

Cade glanced at Brandon as he rode in front of Chance. The boy was grinning as his uncle showed him how his expert cow-horse, Ace, separated the calf from its mama.

Cade's chest swelled seeing his son watch intently Chance's instructions then take over the reins. Of course the horse did most of the work, but Brandon's look of pride was worth a million dollars.

His thoughts turned to Abby.

He looked toward the house, expecting her to be waiting anxiously. There were women busy at the tables that had been set up in the shade. He spotted Abby, and a stirring started low in his gut. She was in jeans and a white blouse. Her red hair was pulled back in a ponytail, though some of those wild curls refused to be tamed. She looked tempting. Too tempting. Like last night. He knew he should never have gone out to the patio. Thank God, he'd ended the kiss when he had. But he didn't know how long his restraint would last. After all, he was only human.

"Hey, get out of the way or get to work!" Chance called.

"Yeah," Brandon said as they rode past him with two calves headed for the pen.

"I guess I'd better. You two are too good for this old city slicker."

Once the Hereford yearlings were inside the fenced area, Chance let Brandon take the reins and walk his horse back to Cade.

"Quite a cowhand you got here," Chance said.

Brandon grinned. "I learn fast."

Cade tapped the boy's dusty hat. "I bet I'm going to catch hel—heck from your mom for bringing you back so dirty."

Brandon shook his head. "Nope, Mom said boys are 'posed to get dirty. It's their job."

Chance pushed his hat back. "Bet you have to take a lot of baths."

Brandon shrugged. "I have to take them, anyway. Mom said I'm dirty no matter if I can see it or not. Is that true, Cade?" Those big brown eyes looked at him. "Is there some dirt you can't see?"

"There is, and your body sweats, too."

"How's come girls don't sweat?" the child asked. "Mom always smells good, like flowers."

Oh, yeah. Abby did smell good. Cade glanced at his

brother as his horse shifted. "I guess that's because men and women are different."

"Different how? I know that girls are softer. They don't have muscles. And when they get older they get breasts." The boy raised his hand to his chest as an example. "But—"

"Look, Brandon, maybe we should save this topic for another time." Cade looked at a grinning Chance and wanted to deck him. "I think we should get cleaned up for lunch."

"Okay." That seemed to satisfy the child. They all dismounted and Brandon tore off toward the house.

Chance gave a deep laugh. "Oh, brother, if you could have seen your face when he said 'breasts.'"

Cade took the reins and led his horse toward the corral. "Just you wait. You have a daughter. That's got to be a lot harder."

"I've got a few more years until I have to worry about Katie. Believe me, I'm going to be watching you closely to see how you handle it all."

Cade socked his brother playfully on the shoulder. "You think I'm going to be around that long?"

Chance grew serious. "I'm planning on it. So is everyone else. I know San Angelo doesn't hold the excitement of Chicago, but you have roots here. Family."

Cade stared at his older brother for a moment. "Sometimes big cities are overrated. My son is here. I want to be around to watch him grow up. But it would be nice if I had a job, so I'm waiting for you to agree to go in on the nature retreat."

"What if I said Joy and I were interested?"

Cade worked to control his excitement. "I'd say we need to talk to Travis."

"Then let's do it," Chance said. "Let's get this show on the road." He slapped his brother on the back. "It's going to be great having you around."

"You may not think that once you see what a slave driver I am. Come on, let's go get some food. I'm starving."

With lunch finally finished, Abby busied herself stacking the dirty plates and flatware to carry inside.

"Are you going to hide out all day?"

Abby turned around to find Cade. He was decked out in his cowboy outfit—jeans, boots, worn leather chaps. He looked good enough to put in an advertisement for the West.

"It takes a lot to feed this crew."

He tipped his hat back. "Well, take a few minutes out to watch Brandon. If it's okay, I'm going to let him help brand."

Abby wiped her hands on her apron. "What do you think? I mean, he's only seven. Some of those big calves could kick and hurt him."

"I'll keep him away until the calf is pinned."

"Who's going to do the roping?"

"I asked Chance."

She nodded. "Good."

He stepped forward. "Abby, this is your ranch. You should be out there."

"You think so?"

"Yes. Several of the men have been asking where you are. Bob Hicks and Matt Henson."

Abby was surprised at the names. "I didn't think Mr. Hicks and Mr. Henson were friends of my father's."

"They didn't come to help Tom Moreau. They're

here for you. As good neighbors. So you should go talk with them."

"I just didn't want to intrude on your time with Brandon."

Cade couldn't believe this conversation. *That* was why Abby was letting him handle things?

"I never wanted you to be excluded. But thank you for being so considerate." He smiled. "Now, grab a hat. The party is down at the pens."

She smiled, and Cade's heart raced. Suddenly he was remembering their kiss two days ago. Last night he'd ached for her again, and by a near miracle, he was able to walk away. He didn't know how many times he could do that.

Abby took off for the house and was back in minutes, minus her apron. She'd put on her old cowboy hat, jammed a pair of work gloves in her back pocket and dug up a small camera. Together they walked down to the holding pens. She went around to each neighbor, thanking them for coming, then helped prepare for the branding.

It had been a while and Cade was a little rusty, but once inside the pen, he remembered how Hank had taught him to flip a calf and hold him down while one ranch hand inoculated and another branded the animal. Within seconds the calf was released and sent back to its mother.

Although Brandon had watched roundups the past couple of years, this was the first time the boy wanted to help. Cade took his son inside the pen but had him stand back until the calf was down. With Cade's help, his son pressed the hot iron against the hide. Nothing prepared him for the smile on Brandon's face when he completed the task.

"Mom, did you see me? I did it. I branded that calf."

"I saw." She held up the camera. "I even got a picture."

"Good. I can show it to Billy at camp. Take one of me and his father." The boy was smiling as he stood next to his father.

"Good idea," Abby said as she snapped another picture.

She continued to use the camera for a few more minutes, then wandered off to talk with a group of the older men.

It didn't take long for Cade to realize he wasn't in shape for this. He'd worked out in Chicago, but he still had trouble keeping up with the other hands. But pride would not allow him to let his son know that he was a softy. He kept going until the last calf wore the Moreau Ranch brand.

Late that evening, Cade groaned as he lowered himself into the spa next to the pool off the patio. Every muscle in his body ached. If he didn't do something now, he didn't think he would be able to climb on his horse tomorrow. That was too embarrassing to think about. Chance would never let him live it down. He closed his eyes and leaned his head back against the edge of the tub.

There was a noise behind him, and he turned to find Abby. She was wearing a blue swimsuit, a short robe covering everything but those damn, long legs.

"Cade. I heard the water, but I didn't know anyone was out here."

He brought his attention to her hair knotted on top of her head. "I was hoping no one would find out," he said. "I guess I'm not exactly in shape for this kind of work."

"Is that so? Not as macho as you thought."

"Woman, I never said I was macho. I just overdid it a little today." His gaze flicked over her, and he wished the robe revealed more. "What are you doing out here?"

"Oh, I couldn't sleep and thought I—"

"You'd sit in the spa for some peace and quiet. And I spoiled that."

"It's okay," she said. "You need it more than I do." She began to back away. "I'll use it another time."

"Hey, you can use it now. There's plenty of room for both of us." Was he crazy? He must be, but he found he would do anything to see her without the cover-up. "Don't be shy."

Abby stiffened. "I'm not. But this isn't a smart idea."

"Figure you can't keep your hands off me, huh?"

With that, Abby jerked her robe off. Cade swallowed. Hard. The royal-blue suit was one piece, but it was cut high on her thighs, nipping in at her narrow waist. Her breasts were full, and he could see the outline of her nipples under the thin fabric. His breathing quickened.

She placed her hands on her hips. "You okay?"

"Yeah, I'm fine."

Abby nodded and sat on the edge of the tub, then swung her legs around. Her mouth opened, and her eyes closed as she sank into the bubbling warm water. "Oh, this is wonderful."

If he didn't know better, he'd think she'd planned this. "Yeah, the water is great."

All at once, her legs slid up against his. She jumped back. "Sorry."

Cade realized the only way he was going to survive this was to get his mind on something else. "I talked with Chance today. He and Joy have agreed to go in on the nature retreat."

"Oh, that's great. Then we can start soon."

He held up a hand. "We still need to talk to Travis. I tried after dinner, but he's a hard man to reach. I'll call again tomorrow." He looked at her across the tub. "You know, this venture is going to take a while to get going."

"I know. Thank goodness you sold the lakefront property, or Brandon and I would have to find another place to live."

Cade glanced away. He'd hoped that the property would have sold before now, but it hadn't. "Well, you don't have to worry about that. Now, with or without Travis's approval, we can move ahead with your side of the project. That is if you still want the cottages built and open for business by next spring."

"I do. But I've been thinking that I should get a job until then. I mean, there's not going to be any extra money coming in."

Cade tensed. He didn't want her out working all day. He needed her here to help with the plans. "You let me worry about the money. Besides, I owe you seven years of back child support. You and Brandon won't want for anything."

She shook her head. "You don't owe me anything, Cade. I'm the one who kept your son from you."

"That's not the point. I want to take care of my family."

"Brandon has had everything he needed."

"Except a father." Cade regretted the words the moment they were out.

He could see by Abby's expression that he'd hurt her.

"I'm sorry," he said.

She didn't say a word as she climbed out of the tub. He had to hurry to catch up with her.

"Abby, wait." He grabbed her arm.

She swung around to him, struggling to break his grip. "Just leave me alone."

"I can't."

They tussled with each other at the edge of the pool, Abby trying to free herself. Suddenly she pushed him and in so doing, toppled backward into the pool.

Cade swore and dived in after her. Ignoring the cold water and sting of chlorine, he helped Abby to the surface.

She gasped for air and pushed her hair from her face. "Look what you did."

"If you would just stop and listen to me."

"I don't want to hear anything you have to say." She pushed him away and swam toward the shallow end. Cade easily caught her.

"Dammit, Abby," he said as he reached for her again. "I'm not letting you go until we talk."

Her breathing was labored as they stood in waist-high water. "Then make it fast."

Cade suddenly lost his voice as his gaze roamed over the upper half of her body. Big mistake. No amount of cold water could keep his own body from responding to her.

"Well, what did you want to say?"

"I'm sorry. I'm sorry I said that to you." He raked

his fingers through his hair. "I don't know what gets into me."

"It's me," she said. "You resent me for keeping Brandon from you. I don't blame you. But I'm not going to let you verbally abuse me." Tears formed in her eyes. "I've spent years listening to someone…" Her words faded as she turned away.

"God, I'm sorry, Abby."

All resistance in him snapped, and he drew her into his arms. She fought him at first, but he coaxed her until finally she gave in and allowed him to draw her body to his. Even in water, he could still smell her special fragrance. Oh, Lord, he wanted her.

"Abby," he whispered as she raised her head, and he could see the surprise and wonder in her eyes. His heart pounded and he didn't think he could take his next breath. He didn't care. He only wanted Abby. His head lowered to hers, then his lips grazed the side of her mouth. He moved to the other side and repeated the action. Then, using his teeth, he gently drew her lower lip into his mouth, sucking gently. She made a whimpering sound as she sagged against him.

"You want more?"

"Yes…"

So did he. A lot more. His lips settled over hers completely, and the torture began. He wanted her to know his pain, and the pleasure they could create together. His kisses grew hungrier, more desperate, until she was clinging to him. He still wanted more. He cupped her breasts in his hands. She quivered as he continued the onslaught of her mouth, pushing his tongue past her teeth until he found hers, then stroked that sweetness until he couldn't stand it any longer.

He broke away. "You're driving me crazy," he said

as his hands moved lower, to her waist, her back, then rose to the straps on her suit. With a gentle tug they came down and exposed her breasts. His breathing all but stopped at the beautiful sight. He lowered his head and closed his mouth over one nipple and suckled until the bud puckered against his tongue.

"Cade…" She gasped and gripped his arms, but didn't stop him. Then her hands began to roam over his chest, followed soon by her lips.

"I want you, Abby," he gasped, and moved her against the side of the pool, pressing his body against hers to let her know how much.

She gasped and stared up at him. The moonlight allowed him to see that her eyes were shimmering with desire. Her lips were swollen from his kisses. She had never looked more beautiful. Words failed him. He reached out, and his fingers caressed her cheek.

Suddenly the sound of men's voices came from alongside the corral. Cade pulled Abby closer, and froze until the intruders walked by just beyond the yard. He could feel her trembling. Finally the voices faded, and he managed to breathe again. The oxygen also brought him back to his senses.

What the hell was he doing practically making love to Abby? If they'd been caught… He pulled her suit back into place.

"I'm sorry. I should never have let things go this far." He caught her hurt look. "I didn't mean it that way. I just don't like the idea of someone walking in on us."

Abby pushed away from him and waded toward the steps at the end of the pool. She was heading up them when Cade decided he couldn't stand to go on like this any longer.

"Don't go, Abby." He started after her. "We need to talk."

"We're always talking, Cade, and it ends up the same. You will always hate me. That will never change."

"I've never hated you, Abby," he said.

"Well, it sure feels like it" She grabbed her robe and put it on. "Look, I can't deal with this now. I know you want to be a part of Brandon's life, and I want that, too. But we're not good together. You resent me. And I can understand that. But this hot and cold..." She stopped and brushed her hair away. "We've got to figure out a way to stay away from each other."

Cade was out of the pool and in front of her. "I don't want it like this, either, Abby."

"Then what do you suggest we do?"

A crazy notion suddenly popped in his head. "Marry me."

Chapter Seven

Abby stared at Cade in disbelief. "Are you crazy?"

"Maybe," he said. "But think about it, Abby." He climbed out of the pool, grabbed a towel off the patio table, then pulled it over his chest. The chest her own hands had caressed only moments ago. Her mouth grew dry, and she jerked her gaze back to his face.

"There's nothing to think about."

"There is when we both want to be a part of Brandon's life," Cade said. "And he needs two parents who love him."

He needs parents who love each other, she cried silently, knowing that the only thing Cade felt for her was resentment. Their life together would be hell. She wouldn't put her son through that, not again. As much as she loved Cade—would always love him—she had to turn him down.

"We can barely stand to be in the same room with each other," she argued.

"That's not what I'd call what was happening in the pool moments ago."

Abby's face heated. She couldn't deny that, not when she could still taste him on her lips, feel his skilled hands on her body. Goose bumps rose on her skin and she crossed her arms. Damn the man. "Just chalk it up to overactive hormones and let it go at that."

His gaze was dark. "It was more than that."

She wanted to believe him. "It would be best if we try to have a cordial relationship—apart—except for raising our son."

"Brandon deserves more," he said. "He needs a family—a mom and dad. I know what that's like, Abby. My dad wasn't around... I don't want that for my son."

Cade stepped closer. She resisted stepping back, recalling the feel of those well-defined muscles under her fingers. Her pulse kicked into overdrive again, but she had to ignore it.

"It would never work, Cade."

"Why not?"

"Well, I think it's obvious." Her voice grew hoarse. "You don't...love me." She held her breath, waiting for his reply.

She caught a flash of pain in his eyes, then he quickly glanced away. "I can take care of you and Brandon financially. Give you a home, make us a family. I'd be committed to you both. And, Abby, you wouldn't ever have to worry about me being unfaithful."

As much as Abby wanted this man, wanted to make a family for their son, a make-believe marriage wasn't the answer. She wanted a real one. And Cade Randell didn't love her.

Tears formed in her eyes. "I can't, Cade. I can't."

Cade watched as Abby ran into the house. His body still ached for her. Once again his heart smarted from her rejection. When would he learn? It wasn't supposed to be like this. He wasn't going to get emotionally involved. Now, once again, he was knee-deep, and he had to stop.

For years he'd tried to bury his feelings for Abby. So when she asked the question about love, he couldn't trust himself to even think about the possibility. There was no doubt he wanted Abby. He just wasn't about to let his heart get involved again.

She wasn't going to be easy to win over. After Garson he wondered if she'd ever trust a man again. And who could blame her? But he wasn't going to let her push him away. Not this time. He was going to have his family.

The next morning when the alarm went off, Abby had wanted to pull the covers over her head and stay in bed. But she couldn't. There were meals to prepare and people to thank for the weekend they gave up to help her.

She'd been thankful Cade stayed away at breakfast. And Brandon, fortunately, seemed content just to watch the goings-on. With only a small herd left to brand, the hands had the calves separated, put into pens and ready to be shipped by early afternoon.

Then everyone sat down to a meal of fried chicken, potato salad and Joy's homemade biscuits. Cade kept his distance, staying close to the other cowboys and Brandon. After the meal, the women cleaned up while the men loaded their horses. Within the hour people were heading out.

Abby waved and called out her thanks as her neighbors drove off. She waited until the dust settled on the road before she turned toward the house. Cade was still there. There was no way to avoid him. She drew a breath and walked inside. The first thing she heard was her son's laughter. When she went into the living room, she found Brandon and Cade wrestling on the floor. She opened her mouth to scold them, but decided it wasn't a big deal. Father and son needed this. She was about to leave, when Brandon spotted her.

"Mom, help me," he begged between giggles. "Cade's too strong." The boy was struggling to get out of his hold.

"Hey, if we're doing teams," Cade said, "I'm calling Chance."

"No!" Brandon cried. "You're both too strong. Mom's only a girl."

"Hey. Wait just a minute." Abby tried not to smile as she came closer. "Girl's aren't all wimps—"

She gasped as Cade's hand grabbed her ankle. Before she could escape, he had her on the floor and pinned beneath him.

"What were you saying about not being a wimp?" he asked, a knowing look in his laughing brown eyes.

"You…you caught me off guard," she managed as his hard body pressed into hers, sending her pulse racing.

"Get used to it, lady." He lowered his head and she could feel his warm breath on her face. "You're not going to get rid of me this time."

Before she could say anything, Brandon climbed on Cade's back. "See, Mom? I told you he's strong."

The boy's weight had pressed Cade even more intimately against her. Cade's eyes were smoldering. Then all too quickly, he moved off her and reached back to make sure Brandon made it safely to the floor.

"I guess we got a little carried away," he admitted as he helped her up. "Did I hurt you?"

She couldn't pull her gaze away. "No, I'm fine. You were gentle enough."

His chest rose with each breath. "I would never intentionally hurt you, Abby."

She swallowed, wanting to believe him. "I know."

"Mom, I'm hungry."

Unable to take her eyes from Cade, she said, "Go ask Carmen for some leftover chicken."

She heard her son scramble out of the room but continued to stand there until Cade spoke. "You've been avoiding me again."

"I've been busy."

"You've been avoiding me," he repeated.

"Okay, I've been avoiding you."

He drew another breath. "I want to spend some time with you, Abby."

"We do spend time together," she said. "You're here with Brandon."

"No, I want to be with you. Just you."

"It's not a good idea, Cade." She wished it was, but it was too late for them.

"Let me show you differently. Go riding with me tomorrow."

"Are you crazy?" She laughed. "You've been in the saddle for two days."

He took her hands in his. "After time in the spa, I felt fine. Come on, say you'll go. I want to show you something."

She couldn't think when he was touching her.
"Okay."

He smiled, then leaned down and placed a lingering
kiss on her mouth. "I'm going to head home now, but
I'll be back early tomorrow. So you'd better be ready
for me."

Abby just stood there as he walked to the door and
left. That was what she was afraid of. She would never
be ready for Cade.

Abby pulled her horse up next to Cade's, and together they looked out over the valley. She drew a
long breath, seeing the beautiful sight. Rich green
grass covered the land, and the hills framed the valley
protectively. There were bushes edging the creek, and
a forest added shade and privacy.

The scene made a perfect picture.

Abby felt her chest tighten, remembering the last
time she'd been here. She'd been with Cade. It was
the day Brandon had been conceived. Anxiety raced
through her. She didn't know if she could handle being
here now. That happy time had been a memory she'd
always cherished. It had helped her through a lot of
bad years.

"It's a beautiful place," Cade said. "I have to say
it's one of the few things I've missed over the years."

"Yes, it's beautiful."

Cade could see that Abby was remembering just as
he was. This valley had been where he and Abby had
come as teenagers. Their relationship had been kept
secret for numerous reasons. The main one had been
her father. Tom Moreau wouldn't allow his daughter
to be seen with a Randell. Cade suspected that had
been one of the reasons Moreau had sent his daughter

away to college. But when she came home, she always rode to the valley—and to him. It had been their place.

He pushed the memory from his head. "Come on," he called as he nudged his horse down the slight slope.

At the creek he climbed off and went to help Abby. He gripped her waist and lifted her from the saddle. Once he set her on the ground, he didn't want to release her, but he forced himself to, afraid he might continue what they'd started the other night.

Abby hadn't helped much in that regard. She looked too tempting in slim black jeans and a fitted peach-colored blouse. She'd let her wild curls cascade around her face. His gaze drifted to her lips, remembering their sweet taste. Realizing the direction of his thoughts, he urged his horse toward the creek.

Abby followed. "Do you think it's a good idea to change all this by letting tourists in?" she asked.

"I'm not going to put any cabins along the creek." He raised his arm and pointed toward the slope. "I thought we'd start with about half a dozen on your side, and my brothers agreed to have the same amount on the Circle B property. They'll be spaced far enough apart to give people plenty of privacy. And all the structures will be hidden in the landscape. Far enough back not to bother the mustangs, but close enough for guests to see nature at its best."

She nodded. "When will this all start, and how soon will we be open for business?"

So, she was interested. "Right away. We should be able to be ready by next spring."

Abby placed her hands on her hips and glanced around. "But how will people get here?"

"From a narrow road off the highway."

She looked at him, her green eyes glowing. "You really think we can make this work?"

He found he liked her use of the pronoun *we*. "I'm investing in it, aren't I?" He went to his horse, untied the blanket and small bag and carried them to a tree deep in the shade. Abby followed.

"But that's what I'm afraid of," she said. "What if this venture fails?"

He spread the blanket and tossed down his hat. "Now don't go and get all nervous on me." He pulled two plastic cups from the sack and went to the creek. Dipping them into the cool water, he returned and offered her a drink. "We're partners."

She sat down on the edge of the blanket and took a drink. "But you're going to be paying for the road and the cabins. I mean, what if—"

He dropped down beside her and put a finger over her lips. "You worry too much. I guess I'm going to have to convince you that you can't expect to get anywhere unless you take some chances." His voice lowered. "I take chances, but I've also gotten a long way on gut instinct. Like now. I feel you need a kiss."

When he pulled her to him and covered her mouth with his, he wasn't thinking about profits and losses. He was thinking how good she felt in his arms. He pushed her back onto the blanket, and Abby didn't resist. She only made a soft sound as her lips parted and he pushed his tongue inside. He stroked and tasted until he nearly went insane with wanting her.

When he ended the kiss, they were both breathing hard. "You're driving me crazy."

Her fingers combed through his hair. "We shouldn't be doing this. I mean, mixing business with... pleasure."

He groaned at her choice of words. "Don't you like the way I touch you?" His hand traced across her face and down her arm, causing her to shiver. "The way I kiss you?" He took gentle nibbles from her mouth until he finally covered her lips completely again.

Abby pushed him away. "Cade, please, we have to stop."

He released her and she sat up. He took a few breaths and composed himself. "Sorry. I guess I let things get out of hand."

He watched as she straightened her hair, tugging the wayward strands behind her ears. She wouldn't look at him. He couldn't stand that.

"Abby."

When she looked at him, her eyes were still dark with desire. He wanted to grin. Instead, he said, "Tell me some ideas you have for the project."

"I haven't thought much about it."

He opened the bag and took out the two sandwiches Ella had packed. He handed her one. "Yes, you have. I noticed you were excited when I was talking earlier."

"Well, I guess I am, a little." She unwrapped the sandwich. "How about a store, a general store? People need to be able to get food staples and have a place to meet for planned outings. And what about souvenirs? I mean you can't go back home without something. I wasn't thinking about tacky souvenirs, but maybe nice collectibles, such as pearls from the Concho River and work from local artists."

Cade was surprised. "You *have* been thinking about this."

She shrugged. "Not exactly, but I wanted to open my own shop after the divorce. Then Dad got sick."

Abby had put her life on hold for others. Maybe he could help her along. "Well, it looks like we'll need another structure for a general store. And a shop for Abby's...Treasures."

Her eyes sparkled in surprise. She started to speak, but he held up his hand.

"Your place will have to be located right by the highway to accommodate local residents, too. And if you acquire some unique items, you can really make a name for yourself, and money."

"I hadn't thought that far ahead," she admitted. "It's just something I've always wanted to do. I loved collecting figurines. My mother gave me several, and I've managed to keep most of them."

Cade wondered if Garson took his anger out on those, too. But he wasn't going to ask her. This was too nice a day to bring up Garson. "Travis finally phoned and gave his okay last week. Even Chance is ready, so I'm going to call in an architect tomorrow. How do you feel about that?"

She released a long breath. "A little scared. All that money. I'm just glad you were able to pay off the bank loan."

He took her hand in his. "I'll never let Joel threaten you again." And she'd never have to know that he himself had bought the lake property. He was betting he could sell it before that happened.

"Have I thanked you for all your help?"

He stared at her for a long time. Abby looked happy. He planned on keeping her that way. "I'm glad you're not avoiding me anymore."

"It would be impossible since you spend so much time with Brandon. And you've stopped asking foolish questions." She played with the crust of her sandwich.

"I don't give up easily, Abby. So enjoy your short reprieve. My proposal still stands."

Her eyes flared. "And I've told you the idea is crazy."

"Not for our son," he said determinedly. "I plan to marry you, Abby. I'm not going away. Not this time."

Later that night Cade's words kept running through Abby's head. *I'm not going away.*

She was lying in bed, unable to sleep. She finally got up and checked on Brandon. Wandering to the kitchen, she made herself a cup of herbal tea, then went back to her room, but nothing could stop her from thinking about Cade. How much she wanted to trust him! But how could she marry a man who didn't love her? He'd just end up resenting her, and they'd be two strangers living in the same house. She couldn't handle that. Not when she loved him.

But his touch was so irresistible, and his kisses weakened her. His incredible smile made it nearly impossible for her think. She didn't know if she could hold out.

And she ached to give her son his father, a family. She found herself wondering if they *could* make it work. Could Cade ever feel something for her again?

"Mom...Mom..." Brandon cried out.

Abby jumped up and grabbed her robe, slipping it on as she hurried down the hall and into her son's room. She found him doubled over, clutching his middle. Lifting him in her arms, she carried him to the bathroom. They just made it to the toilet before he emptied his stomach.

Afterward, she wiped off his face, then Brandon

collapsed in her arms and began to cry. "My stomach hurts bad."

"Oh, honey. You must have eaten something that didn't agree with you."

Brandon groaned again, and Abby led him back to the toilet. "It hurts."

"I know, baby." She smoothed her son's forehead, and quickly realized he had a fever. All at once her concern grew. Maybe this wasn't just an upset stomach.

"Brandon, where does it hurt?"

"All over. My throat. My stomach hurts real bad."

She reached for a towel from the rack, laid her son down on the bathroom rug and covered him.

"I'm going to call the doctor."

"Please, I want Cade."

Abby was surprised at Brandon's request, but she stood her ground. "I need to talk to a doctor first, then I'll call Cade." Maybe it was a good idea. A father should be involved in all aspects of his child's life. She dashed to the phone in her room and called Brandon's pediatrician, then punched out the number to the Circle B and had Hank give Cade the message that his son was ill and was asking for him.

Fifteen minutes later Cade raced up the gravel drive to the Moreau ranch. He braked the truck at the front of the house and jumped out. He was tucking in his shirt as he ran to the porch where Abby, dressed in a robe, swung open the door. He saw the worried look on her face.

"I got here as soon as I could," he said. "How's Brandon?"

"He's upstairs. I'm scared, Cade. He's still clutching his stomach. The doctor said to take him to the emergency room.''

He gripped her by the shoulders. ''Then we better do it.''

She bit her trembling lip and nodded.

Cade took the steps two at a time and rushed into the bathroom. His son lay on the rug next to the toilet. He looked so fragile and helpless. Cade swallowed back his fear and forced a smile. ''Hey, partner, I hear you ate something that didn't agree with you.''

Brandon raised his head and was immediately racked with dry heaves. Cade went to him and held him in his arms until the heaving subsided.

''I'm not a baby, Cade…but it hurts.''

He touched his son's ashen face and felt unbearably helpless. ''You're a lot braver than I would be. Maybe we should go to the doctor and see if he can give you something.''

'''Kay,'' Brandon said, closing his eyes. ''You take me.''

''You bet,'' Cade said as he glanced at Abby, standing in the bathroom doorway.

''I'll get dressed.'' She hurried off.

Five minutes later they were on their way to the hospital. Surprisingly the emergency room was pretty quiet, and the doctor on call examined Brandon within thirty minutes. All the while Cade never left Brandon's side.

After tests were completed, the doctor announced that Brandon had a stomach virus. He prescribed a medication to help control the vomiting and told them to take him home. Both he and Abby were relieved. At the desk Abby used her insurance card to pay the bill then hurried back to Brandon.

Cade lifted the seven-year-old in his arms, and they headed out to the truck.

After a quick stop by the pharmacy, they drove back home. Abby gave Brandon a dose of the medicine, and Cade took him upstairs and settled him in bed. Five minutes later the child was asleep.

Still hesitant to go, Cade finally decided it was safe to leave the boy's side. He'd most likely sleep until morning. After placing a kiss on his son's forehead, Cade walked out into the hall. Abby followed and closed the door. Together they went downstairs.

Abby looked at him, tears clouding her eyes. "I'm sorry I panicked."

"Shh," Cade said, and pulled her into his arms. He knew that they were both thinking how lucky they were that Brandon wasn't seriously ill. "Never hesitate to call me. God, I love that boy." His hold tightened on her, then he released her. "Abby, I can't stand this anymore. I need to be in Brandon's life. I want him to know he's my son. That I'm his father."

She looked worried. "Please, Cade, you promised you would wait."

He glared at her. "Not for much longer. I've been more than fair about giving you time. I want Brandon to know I'm his father."

"I know, but I'm not sure how he'll react. He's just a child."

Cade nodded. He knew he had to think about Brandon. Would the boy accept him? "Okay, I'll wait, but I'm going to sleep on the sofa tonight in case Brandon wakes up and needs something."

"There's no need, Cade," she said, hurrying after him. "I'll be sleeping in the next room. Besides, what will people think?"

He stopped in front of the sofa and swung around. "Dammit, Abby, who's going to know? Charlie…Carmen." He raked a hand through his hair. "You know, it wouldn't have to be this way if you'd just marry me."

Her back stiffened. "Wow, how can a girl turn down such a wonderful proposal? I can. Good night, Cade." She turned and marched out of the room, leaving him to wonder why she could still get to him. The stirring in his gut told him how much he wanted her. Abby still wanted him, too. Wasn't that attraction enough?

She sure as hell wasn't getting his heart again.

Chapter Eight

Cade groaned and rolled over, trying again to get comfortable on the cramped sofa, which was impossible sleeping in jeans. Giving up, he opened his eyes to discover a pair of big, brown ones staring back at him, over a small nose sprinkled with freckles and a smiling mouth, exposing a space where a tooth had once been. Brandon.

"Oh, boy, you're awake," the child said. "Mom said I had to be quiet 'cause you need your sleep."

Cade propped himself on one elbow, noticing the seven-year-old's coloring was back to normal. "What time is it?"

Brandon glanced over at the clock on the mantel. "It's ten minutes after eight. You slept a long time."

"You should have woken me." Cade swung his legs to the floor and sat up. After rubbing his eyes, he glanced at his son, then around the empty living room. "Have you seen him?"

"Who?" Brandon asked.

"The boy who was so sick last night. Did you see where he went?"

Brandon stood up with a big grin. "It's me!" he said, thumbing his chest. "I'm all better today."

Cade gasped. "You can't be him," he said. "The kid I remember was puking his guts out."

Brandon wrinkled his nose. "Gross, huh?"

"So how are you feeling this morning?"

"Good. Mom says it's a miracle."

Cade couldn't be more tickled about Brandon's quick recovery.

"You want some breakfast?" the boy asked. "I already ate some toast. Mom makes the best pancakes. I couldn't have any, but you can if you want."

He was hungry. "I don't want to make extra work for your mom."

"You won't. She was fixin' 'em when I came in here." He pulled on Cade's arm until he stood. "C'mon, you can only eat in here if you're sick."

"I guess that leaves us out."

Cade followed Brandon into the kitchen, but he wasn't prepared for what he found. Abby in the morning. She looked fresh and pretty in her honey-colored blouse and long skirt. Her hair was pulled back from her face, shiny clips holding it in place. Her green eyes were bright. Suddenly his tired body came to life.

"Good morning," she said, and handed him a cup of coffee. "What else can I get for you?"

Cade took a much-needed sip and nearly choked. He doubted she was offering what he wanted. "Whatever you're fixing is fine."

Abby tried not to stare when Brandon brought Cade into the room. For a man who'd been up half the night, he looked way too good. Short dark stubble covered his jaw. His hair was messed up and his brown eyes were hooded. Now she understood what was meant by the phrase *bedroom eyes.* His shirt hung open, exposing his powerful chest. Wicked thoughts rushed into her head. She remembered how she'd had to fight last night to keep herself from joining him downstairs.

"Mom, Cade wants pancakes."

Her son's voice jolted her back to reality. "Oh, right."

"You don't have to fix my breakfast," Cade insisted.

"It's the least I can do after all you did for us." She turned on the griddle and reached for the bowl of batter.

"Yeah, Cade, you came over 'cause I was sick," Brandon said. "We want to thank you. So you gotta eat."

"Yes, you have to eat," Abby repeated. "And I might be persuaded to give one small pancake to a certain young man if he washes his hands."

"All right," Brandon said as he rushed out of the kitchen.

Bad idea. Now she was alone with Cade. But before she could gather the words to call her son back, he was gone. She turned quickly and busied herself at the stove.

Cade came up behind her. "You look awfully pretty this morning." He leaned closer, his breath caressing her neck, then her ear, causing a warm shiver to move down her spine.

"The wonderful advantage of makeup. It hides the dark circles."

"You still look beautiful." This time he placed a kiss on her neck.

Abby gasped, but didn't pull away. "You shouldn't do that."

"I can't help myself. You're just too tempting standing here."

So are you, Abby thought. "Brandon could come in…"

Cade turned her around to look at him. "So what? He'll see me kissing his mother. Do you want me to kiss you, Abby? When you went to bed last night, were you aching for me like I was aching for you?"

"Oh, Cade."

"Hey, Mom," Brandon came running into the room, then stopped suddenly. His rounded eyes went from her to Cade. "Are you kissing like Chance and Joy?"

Heat rushed to Abby's face and she pulled away. "No, we're going to sit down and eat breakfast." She poured some batter on the griddle. "Then you're going to take it easy today and play inside."

"Aw, Mom," Brandon climbed into a chair. "Can't I go riding?"

"No. Not until I'm sure you're really better."

"But it's so boring in the house."

"Hey, Bran," Cade said as he came around the table and pulled out a chair. "Why don't I hang out with you? I mean, I have to run back to the Circle B and shower and change, but you can go with me if it's all right with your mom."

Both Cade and Brandon turned their identical gazes on her. "Can I, Mom?" her son asked.

She felt a twinge of envy as she busied herself flipping the pancakes. She wanted so much for father and son to have a relationship, but it was hard to let go. "Let's see how you feel after a pancake."

Brandon rewarded her with a smile. "You're the best mom in the whole world."

Was she? Had keeping her son from his father been the right thing to do? Would Brandon forgive her? Emotions welled up inside her, and she swallowed hard. "You say that every time you get your way."

Abby scooped the pancakes off the griddle and heard her son's sweet giggle. Filling the plates, she carried them to the table, catching Cade's gaze as he mouthed, "Thank you."

Abby didn't have any choice. She was now officially sharing her son with Cade.

The house was quiet all morning. Too quiet. Abby busied herself helping Carmen strip the beds and do the laundry. Around noon she ended up in the study dusting and polishing the furniture. She glanced at the neat stacks of papers on her father's desk and decided not to mess with Cade's work. Not that he had been denying her access to any business information. He had shown her the receipt for the cattle sale, and another sizable check had come in to pay for Dancer's stud fee. Abby had tried to distance herself, but it hadn't worked. There was no way around it—she couldn't avoid the man.

Cade had been in the house every day since he'd agreed to help her with the ranch's financial troubles. She also knew most of that time had been so he could be with his son. But with Cade Randell around so much, how long could she keep her feelings hidden?

Abby closed her eyes and thought back to her weak moments, what had happened in the pool, then again at Mustang Valley. How close they'd come... She shivered, remembering Cade's touch, his caresses.

Kisses that had driven her crazy. She drew a breath as a stirring erupted deep within her stomach.

She was in love with the man. Abby doubted she had ever stopped loving him. Cade had proposed twice, saying he wanted them to be a family.

But how could she marry him, knowing he didn't love her? What if, later on, Cade found someone else and truly fell in love? Would he just leave her and Brandon? Tears formed in her eyes. She couldn't handle it. She couldn't lose him a second time.

The sound of the front door opening brought her out of her thoughts. Then she heard Brandon's voice as he and Cade came into the study.

"Oh, Mom, I had so much fun. I saw Princess Star again. She's getting big. She remembered me, too…" Brandon stopped. "Mom, you crying?"

Abby shook her head, refusing to look at Cade. "No, just something in my eye." She touched her son's flushed cheek. "Hey, I thought you were supposed to take it easy today."

"I did. I played cards with Hank. He taught me five-card stud."

Abby's gaze shot to Cade.

"Don't worry," Cade said. "I doubt a few hands of cards will turn Brandon into a gambler."

Her gaze went back to her child. "Did you have lunch?"

Brandon nodded and tried to hide a yawn. "Ella fixed us some soup."

"Well, I think being up all night has caught up with you," she said. "Time for a little nap."

"Aw, Mom, I'm not a baby."

"I know, but you were sick."

"Come on, partner," Cade said as he lifted the boy

in his arms. Brandon didn't fight, but instead, laid his head on Cade's shoulder. "I'll take you upstairs. I don't want to have to drive you back to the hospital."

"'Kay," Brandon answered.

Cade winked at Abby and headed out of the room. She watched with an ache in her heart. Brandon had taken to Cade almost immediately. Her son had been so starved for a father. Maybe it was one thing she could give him.

Cade returned a few minutes later. "Brandon was asleep before I got his shoes off." He leaned a hip against the desk. "I wanted to stay and just watch him. He's amazing. So full of curiosity. I didn't mean to tire him out, but he was so eager to go see everything."

Abby looked at Cade. She noticed he'd shaved and changed into fresh black jeans and a wine-colored polo shirt. "It's never been easy to tell Brandon no. He's so sweet. Always has been. Even as a baby he was good."

Cade's gaze locked with hers. "Do you think I could see his baby pictures?"

"Of course. I'll give you some albums to take home. You can keep any you want."

Cade found that his anger at Abby had been subsiding in the past few days. Baby photos weren't going to change anything, but hanging on to negative feelings wouldn't, either. At least now he could be with his son. And the more time he spent with Brandon, the more he realized how blessed he was to have this child. All he wanted to do was concentrate on making a life with the boy…and Abby. But Cade knew that was going to take some time.

"You want to go for a walk?" he asked. "It's too nice a day to stay inside."

She looked surprised. "Sure."

Cade took Abby's hand, and they walked through the house to the kitchen to tell Carmen that Brandon was napping. She grabbed a sun hat and together they walked out into the sunny afternoon. It was hot, but not more than usual for a Texas summer day. Silently they made their way toward the barn and corral.

"Does Brandon miss Midnight Dancer?" Cade asked.

"He hasn't said a whole lot," Abby confessed. "You've had him pretty busy lately with the roundup and all."

"I wanted to take him to Chance's place today, but I was afraid I'd wear him out."

"I can tell he loved every minute of the morning. You've been such a good influence on him."

Cade laughed. "I bet your daddy wouldn't feel that way."

Abby stole a glance at him as they went into the barn. The sudden dimness made her blink, and it took a moment for her eyes to adjust. "My daddy never knew you like I did."

The last thing Cade wanted was to get into a long discussion about Tom Moreau, so he changed the subject. "I managed to talk with an architect this morning. We've set up a meeting for tomorrow. Is that convenient for you?"

Abby looked surprised. "That's fine. Thank you for including me."

"I wouldn't ever exclude you. Not from the business or my time with Brandon. I meant what I said, Abby. I want us to be partners. Most of all I want us to be a family." He stopped and took her by the arms. "I also want to be with you."

Her eyes filled with tenderness. "I want that, too," she admitted in a whisper.

Cade's heart swelled. Finally. "You do?"

She nodded slowly. "I'm scared, Cade, but I want us to share Brandon's life."

"Does that mean you'll marry—"

She raised a hand. "I can't say, not now." She closed her eyes. "My marriage to Joel was a disaster, but I can't put all the blame on him. I don't want to rush into anything." Her green eyes searched his face. "Could we maybe…date to see if…"

His pulse raced. "I'd like that." He smiled. "I love my son, but there are times I'd like to be alone with you."

She laughed. "Welcome to parenthood."

He leaned forward and placed a kiss on her inviting mouth. "After the meeting with architect tomorrow, I promised Brandon I'd take him riding. But we'll be back by supper. How would you like to go out to dinner?"

"Just you and me? I'd like that."

He couldn't resist kissing her again. This time he wrapped his arms around her, dragging her closer. Finally he released her. "Whoa, I think we better stop before things get out of hand."

"That seems to happen a lot with us," Abby said, looking away as if embarrassed.

He touched her cheek and made her look at him. "There's nothing wrong with the way we feel."

She drew a long breath. "It scares me sometimes."

"I'd never hurt you, Abby."

"I know." Her voice became husky. "I remember...how gentle you were, how loving."

And as hard as he'd tried over the years, he hadn't been able to forget, either. He pulled her close. "I remember, too."

Cade dressed in a dark business suit, a snowy-white shirt with a paisley tie and the usual Texan footwear—boots. Shiny black custom-made boots.

He was the picture of success, Abby thought as they sat with the architect going over the plans for the retreat. They wanted a unique design for their cabins, something that fit in with the landscape and was private enough to attract everything from nature hikers to newlyweds. Once satisfied that James Nyce was their man, their next stop was a civil engineer, who would survey the land.

Instead of driving home, Cade headed to Chance's ranch to talk with him and Joy. They needed to know what was happening.

When Cade and Abby pulled into the drive, Joy came out to meet them. She ran down the steps.

"What a surprise." She hugged Cade, then Abby. "Where's Brandon?"

Cade had removed his tie and suit jacket. "He's at home with Carmen. We thought we'd let you know about our meetings this morning. Is Chance around?"

"He's in the barn. Come on inside and I'll call him."

They walked through the yard, where they were greeted by the family's Labradors, Sunny and Ginger. When Joy finally shooed the dogs away, Abby and Cade followed her inside.

"Excuse the mess," she said. "We still haven't finished in here. Seems everything I selected had to be back-ordered. For now, you'll have to use your imagination.''

Abby looked around the kitchen. New whitewashed cabinets were up, but the countertops were sheets of plywood, the floor the same. "It's going to look beautiful when it's finished,'' she said.

"One can always hope," Joy said. "Please, sit down.'' She directed them to the scarred maple table, then went to the phone, punched in a number and waited. "Honey, your brother and Abby are here. Sure." She hung up. "He'll be here in a minute. How about some coffee?''

"Sounds great," Cade said.

Joy went to the cupboard and pulled down four mugs. "And you're staying for lunch, so don't even argue. Seems like forever since I've seen you two. I hear Brandon was sick, and you had to take him to the emergency room.''

"It turned out to be stomach flu.''

Joy frowned. "Anytime your child is sick, it's scary.''

Abby knew that was true, but the look on Cade's face that night had surprised her. He'd been just as afraid as she'd been.

"This parenting stuff is all new to me," Cade said. "I wish there was a class to go to.''

Chance walked in the back door. He was dressed in faded jeans and chaps. He smiled and Abby could see the strong Randell-family resemblance. "So you came over to ask for advice on how to be a great dad?''

"Very funny," Cade said. "You don't have that much experience. A few months.''

He kissed Joy. "More than you.''

Cade smiled then. "Everyone has more than me. But I'm learning fast."

Chance brought his coffee to the table and sat down. "That's the secret, bro—you got to keep one step ahead of them."

They all laughed.

"Why don't we continue this over lunch?" Joy suggested.

Abby helped Joy prepare the meal while Chance and Cade went over the progress of the project. The women voiced their opinions when needed. As they were finishing up the discussion, Abby heard Katie wake up from her nap. She offered to go get her.

After Joy fed her, she handed her back to Abby.

Cade watched in wonder as the two got acquainted. He was amazed at how easily Abby held and talked to the baby. She was the picture of motherhood.

"Oh, I miss this stage," Abby said. "They're so cute. They smile and coo at everything you say. Their eyes follow you everywhere." As if cued, Katie began making sounds and waving her arms.

Joy came up beside her. "I'm kind of waiting for the stage when they entertain themselves more. I can't seem to get anything done when she's awake. She sleeps through the night, though." Joy took the baby from Abby and went to Cade. "I think Katie and her uncle Cade need some time together."

Cade wasn't prepared when she nearly dumped the pink bundle in his arms. "Hey, wait. How do I do this?"

"Figure it out, Uncle. Come on, Abby," Joy said. "I want to show you my newly decorated bedroom." As they started out of the kitchen, Joy turned. "You guys think you can handle things while we're gone?"

"Piece of cake," Chance said and waved them off.

Cade looked down at little Katie and found her staring up at him. He thought she was going to cry when her face turned all red, then the usually sweet bundle took on a new odor, and not a pleasant one. "Ah, Chance, I think we have an emergency here."

His brother leaned over, caught a whiff and began to laugh. "I guess the little princess has finally initiated you. Come on, Cade." Chance stood. "I'll show you what you missed with Brandon."

At this late date Cade wasn't all that sure he wanted to experience it. But what choice did he have? He doubted his brother was going to let him just watch.

Joy escorted Abby into the beautiful master suite. The off-white carpeting was plush and set off the huge mahogany four-poster bed. A burgundy comforter adorned the mattress, along with navy and cream toss pillows stacked against the headboard. The windows were covered with wooden blinds, and two Tiffany lamps sat on tables on either side of the bed.

"This is lovely."

Joy went to the double doors that led into the nursery. "When Katie is a little older, Chance wants to turn this room into a master bath."

"That'll be wonderful." What Abby envied wasn't the home as much as the relationship Joy and Chance had. It was obvious how much the couple loved each other. Abby could see it every time they were together.

"It's Chance who's been wonderful," Joy said as she sat down on the bed and motioned for Abby to join her. "You know our marriage didn't start out in exactly a conventional way. But when we discovered our true feelings, we renewed our vows and decided to make this house our home. It was Chance's idea to redecorate this room first. He said it was a new beginning for us.'' Joy's blue eyes locked with Abby's. ''You can tell me it's none of my business, but what's going on between you and Cade?''

Abby blinked at the blunt question. ''Well, we're working on the project...to help save the ranch for Brandon.''

''That not what I meant. I have an idea of what that man has on his mind when he can't keep his eyes off you. And Cade's not thinking about his son when he looks at you.''

''Cade and I realize...there're still a lot of feelings between us. But we have issues, and the major one is that I didn't tell him about Brandon...'' Abby took a long breath. ''I don't think Cade can ever completely forgive me.''

Joy studied her. ''I know how stubborn the Randell men can be. Chance put me though a lot. And he'd probably still be holding back if I hadn't forced the issue. I found my opportunity, let him know how I felt, then I seduced him.''

Abby smiled. ''That's not our problem. Cade wants to marry me. He wants us to make a home for Brandon.''

Joy arched an eyebrow. ''And this is a bad thing?''

''It is if the man you love can never return that love.''

''Then work through it together. Marriages have started on a lot less. Look at Chance and me. He didn't even like me at first. He'd planned on buying this ranch when I showed up to claim it as the only heir.

''Then he figured he could get me to sell out, and when the Randell men want something, they go after it.'' A smile appeared on her face. ''And I'm awfully glad he did. He's a loving husband and father. He adores Katie as if she's his own. And as far as I'm concerned, Chance is her father.'' Joy paused. ''I mean it, Abby. When it comes to love, sometimes you have to convince the man that you're the only woman for him.''

Abby wanted to share Joy's enthusiasm, but it was difficult. ''What if you're wrong about Cade?''

Joy shook her head. ''I'm telling you, Abby, Cade Randell loves you. He's just not ready to admit it yet.''

True or not, Abby doubted that Cade would ever admit it to himself, let alone to her.

Chapter Nine

Cade was pulling on his boots when he heard a knock on his bedroom door.

Ella called out. "You decent?" she asked.

Cade grinned. "There's some people around here would say I never was."

The Circle B housekeeper peered inside, then walked in carrying a freshly ironed white shirt. "They didn't know what a sweet boy you were underneath all that anger," she said.

"You're one of a kind, Ella. Thanks." Cade took the shirt and kissed the woman on the cheek.

For as long as he could remember, Ella had worn jeans and a serviceable cotton blouse. In the winter she switched to a plaid flannel shirt. Over the years her dark hair had turned gray, but she still wore the same no-nonsense clothing.

"How did you ever handle three hoodlums?" Cade repeated one of the many names the Randell boys had been called by the community.

She waved her hand. "You three weren't all that tough. Once Hank and I straightened out the trouble other people caused, all you and your brothers needed was some love." Her voice lowered with emotion. "And I was lucky, because I got a lot back in return. So don't go thinkin' raising you boys was only a chore. There were many benefits. Now that you have a son, you'll understand what I mean." She shook her head and smiled. "You and Chance, daddies. Now, don't that beat all. So when are you going to bring that young man around so we can spoil him?"

Cade fastened the snaps on his shirt. "Soon, I hope, but you'll have to get in line behind me."

"I just bet Abby might have something to say about that."

Cade had no doubt Abby was a good mother, but all he wanted was a chance to be a good father. If she would let him. "You're right, she does." He sighed. "All I want is to tell Brandon I'm his father. Abby wants to wait a little longer."

Ella pursed her lips. "That's not an easy thing to tell a seven-year-old. Brandon hasn't done too well in the daddy department. After losing his grandfather so recently, maybe a little more time wouldn't hurt."

That wasn't what Cade wanted to hear. "It's killing me. I want Brandon to know I'm his father."

"He will. Remember, Cade, you've only been home a short time. Just let Brandon know you're going to be here for him, that you love him. That's what that child needs right now."

Cade didn't like it, but he had to agree. He remembered, back when his daddy had been arrested for rustling, how the kids in school teased him and his brothers ruthlessly. How many fights he'd gotten into. He'd used his fists to try to erase the pain, the loneliness, the shame.

Cade's thoughts went to Hank's birthday party and how fierce Brandon got when he thought someone was threatening his mother. Had his son learned to fight because of Garson's abuse? Would it get worse when he became a Randell?

"Ella, I want my son to have my name."

She smiled. "Of course you do."

"But but there are still people out there who hate the Randells. Tom Moreau was one of them."

She raised an eyebrow. "So that's what has you bothered."

Cade nodded.

"Well, all I can say is what Hank told you boys years ago when you first came to the Circle B. You aren't your daddy, and don't let people make you think you're like him." Ella's eyes watered. "Cade, you've worked hard to get where you are. You are a good honest man, and any child would be proud to have you for his daddy."

Emotion clogged Cade's throat as he pulled the older woman into a tight embrace. "Oh, Ella, I've missed you." He kissed her cheek again.

"Well, you're not going to miss me anymore. You're home where you belong."

Was he? Could he make a home for Brandon—and a life with Abby? Could he forgive and forget? It still stung that she had chosen Garson over him and kept Brandon from him. He wanted Abby in the worst way, but he couldn't risk his heart.

As if Ella could read his mind, she touched his arm. "You've got to let go of the past, Cade. It's not going to do you any good to beat it into the ground. You can't change a thing. Just like you can't change your feelings for Abby."

He tried to protest, but she raised her hand.

"You're not foolin' anyone, Cade Randell. So get rid of your anger and go after that girl."

"I've already asked her to marry me. She told me it wouldn't work."

"Then you must've been doin' it wrong." Ella crossed her arms. "So figure out the right way to do it."

Cade grinned. "I'm trying my best." He turned toward the dresser mirror to examine his attire, a western-cut shirt and new black jeans and boots.

"See that you do." The housekeeper sighed as she stood behind him, glancing into the same mirror. "Well, if looks count for anything, you and your brothers have always been the most handsome boys in the county. Though it wouldn't hurt to remember some of that Texas charm when you're out tonight."

He cocked an eyebrow. "Yes, ma'am."

"And make sure Abby knows that you're here to stay."

Cade turned around. He'd enjoyed being home this past month. He hadn't even known how much he'd missed everyone. "I'm not going anywhere. I'm home."

Two hours later Cade parked the truck on the side of the street and went around to help Abby out. She thanked him as she stepped down on to the pavement of historic Concho Avenue.

It was his pleasure, he thought as he eyed her violet sundress with its full skirt. She had on rope-soled sandals that strapped around her slim ankles, accenting her long gorgeous legs.

Abby's hair was in curls and danced freely around her face. When he leaned close to her, his nostrils were teased by the soft scent of her perfume. "I hope you don't mind if we play tourist tonight," he said.

"I don't mind." She smiled. "Gosh, I haven't been here in years."

Cade took her hand as they stepped up onto the wooden sidewalk and strolled by the restored century-old storefronts. "You know, even though I went to college in town, I never made it over here. Guess I thought it wouldn't be very interesting."

Her green eyes raised to his. "And now?"

"I'll probably discover more about where I live. I mean, what if Brandon needs help on a school project about local history? Think we should take him on the Heritage Trail, Fort San Angelo and the riverwalk?"

"Not all in one day, but they could be fun outings."

Cade nodded, finding himself suddenly awkward with Abby. Damn. He didn't like it. He'd always prided himself on being able to handle himself in any situation. Now he was stumbling around like a teenager.

Silently they passed by tourists going in and out of the stores that lined the street, then finally reached Miss Hattie's Bordello Museum.

Abby laughed. "I don't think Brandon needs to know about this."

"I think we can hold off for a few years. Come on." Cade tugged on her arm and walked her two doors down to Miss Hattie's Café and Saloon.

"Oh, I've never been here," Abby said excitedly.

"Neither have I. So this is another first for us."

"Another?"

"This is our first date," Cade reminded her. He raised their clasped hands to his lips and placed a kiss on her fingers. "I never got the chance to actually take you out before."

Her eyes grew dark with desire. "Oh, I guess it is," she said, her voice throaty.

Suddenly he wondered if he was doing this all wrong. "Maybe I should have taken you some place fancy, but I thought we could have a quiet dinner, then maybe take a walk along the river...."

She rested her hand on his arm. "Cade, it's perfect."

She was the one who was perfect. He couldn't take his eyes off her face, her flawless ivory complexion and full inviting mouth. Her eyes simmered with passion, pulling him into their shimmering green depths. He lost all sense of time, couldn't figure out how to take his next breath. Someone on the sidewalk bumped him, bringing him out of the trance. "I guess we should go inside," he said.

They stepped through the double cut-glass doors and stood in awe of the shotgun-style building with its white rock walls and hardwood floors.

Cade took Abby into the dimly lit bar. Candle lamps flickered on small, intimate tables. Several antiques adorned the area, but what drew most people's attention was the large portrait of the notorious Miss Hattie hanging on the tapestry-covered wall.

"Oh, Cade. This is nice."

His hold on her hand tightened. "I'm glad you like it."

Cade escorted her to a quiet table. A waitress appeared for their drink order.

"What would you like?" he asked Abby.

"Just a ginger ale."

A light went on in Cade's brain. "I'll have the same," he told the waitress. "We'll order later." He turned back to Abby. "I'm sorry. I didn't think that bringing you to a bar... I mean, with Joel's drinking problem."

Abby smiled, touched by Cade's concern. He'd been trying so hard to please her. "And that's what it is, Joel's problem," she assured him. "I never drink much—just a little wine—but that's only because I don't like the taste."

His dark eyes captured her as he reached out and took her hand. "You amaze me," he said. "You've been through so much and you just handle it."

Oh, no, she didn't always handle it. He hadn't seen her two years ago when she'd been at the lowest point in her life. Not when she had allowed a man to use her as a punching bag. She drew a deep breath and shook off the brutal memory. "Brandon is my anchor and inspiration. You can't give up when you have a child depending on you."

Cade's gaze grew intense. "God, Abby, I wish I'd been there for you."

How many times had she wished the same thing? How many times had she regretted not calling Cade back that day eight years ago and telling him she was pregnant?

"We can't change the past, Cade," she said. "We've both made mistakes." Her eyes brimmed. "But if I could, I would—"

Just then the waitress arrived with their drinks. After she walked away, Cade scooted his chair closer to Abby. "No, Abby, don't cry." He leaned forward and took her hands. "You're right. We can't go back. But just so you know, I'm always going to be here for you and Brandon."

Abby blinked. She didn't want tears to spoil their night. Nothing could make her happier than seeing Brandon and Cade build a strong relationship. "Our son is at that age where he needs a father."

"I'll do my best." Cade laced their fingers together. "And just so you know, I'm staying in San Angelo permanently." He winked. "And I'm going to win you back. I'm going to make you trust again."

Abby lost the ability to breathe.

"We can make a good life together," he continued. "You, me and Brandon."

Abby had to look away from the promise she saw in Cade's eyes, so she studied the condensation on her glass. "Be careful what you commit to, Cade. You had a life in Chicago for a lot of years. You may want to go back."

"No. I had an existence. I've already resigned from my job," he said. "I will need to go back and pack up my things, and put my condo on the market."

"It is that easy for you?" she asked. "You can just break all your ties and walk away?"

He frowned. "I don't have many ties." He shrugged. "A few friends from the office. Of course, I have a lot of business contacts, but I can stay in touch. If you're worried about me financially, I assure you, I'll do fine. I've made some good investments over the years that will help."

Abby couldn't care less about his financial position. "There isn't anyone special?" she finally asked, needing to know.

"Special? As in a woman?" He smiled again. "Oh, my, the lady is jealous."

"I am not," she denied just as he leaned close and planted a lingering kiss on her lips. Sparks shot through her, ending low in her stomach. When he pulled back, she nearly moaned in frustration.

"You were saying?" he asked with a wicked gleam in his eye.

"I'm not jealous." Her voice was breathy.

His eyes held hers. "And there's no reason you should be."

"But you've been gone a long time."

He grew serious. "A while back there was someone. But we never got to the marriage stage. I was too busy with my career. She got tired of me breaking dates because of work." His fingers caressed the sensitive skin on her arm, and Abby felt warm tingles spread through her. "It's taken me a long time to realize what's important to me." His look was dark and penetrating. "It's you and Brandon."

Abby wanted to believe him. She'd loved Cade Randell for so long.

He leaned close again. "Do you have any idea how badly I want you?"

Her gaze shot to his, and she soon discovered the smoldering fire in his eyes. Her heart began to drum.

Before Abby could find her voice, the waitress appeared with menus, and their concentration turned to the meal.

When once again they were alone, Cade took her hand again. "I can't seem to stop touching you," he said. "I don't want to let go."

"I don't want you to," she admitted, enjoying the gentleness of his touch.

Cade linked his fingers through hers. "Be careful, Abby, I may just kidnap you and have my way with you."

Abby couldn't answer as their heated gazes locked. Soon both were unaware of anything but each other. Not the noise or people mingling around them. It had always been this way between them.

When the food arrived, they tried to keep the conversation light, discussing where they'd go on their second date, but things were simmering underneath.

Soon Cade's food grew tasteless. He put down his fork and noticed Abby had done the same. The heated desire in her eyes mirrored his feelings. Cade wanted nothing more than to take Abby in his arms.

But he knew he had to go slowly. They both needed to cool off. "How about a walk by the river?" he suggested, knowing he didn't want to go home yet.

"I'd like that," she said.

"Good." He glanced around for the waitress. Getting her attention, he already had his money out of his wallet when she arrived at the table. He gave her a big tip, then helped Abby from her chair. With his hand on her waist, he guided her toward the exit, promising himself that the second he was outside, she was going to be in his arms

Feeling like a giddy teenager, Abby asked for directions to the ladies' room. "I'll meet you at the front door," she said as she broke away, hoping that Cade hadn't noticed her nervousness. She hadn't been on a date since…forever. It was crazy, but she wanted to relive those lost years with Cade.

After checking her makeup, she'd just left the rest room and was headed for the door when she heard a familiar voice. Immediately she stiffened, then felt a hand on her shoulder.

"Well, well, if it isn't the little wife," Joel said.

Abby tried to get out of the narrow hallway and away from her ex-husband. She knew from past experience that Joel loved to make trouble. She searched the area with her gaze in hopes that Cade wasn't too far away, but there was no sign of him.

Abby realized she'd have to do this on her own. She turned to face the man who'd made her and her son's life a living hell. He looked terrible. No suit coat, and his white shirt was wrinkled and dirty. But his bloodshot eyes were what gave away that he'd been drinking. Abby started to shake with fear, and clenched her fists to fight it. "I'm not your wife anymore, Joel, so leave me alone."

Anger flashed across his ruddy face, and he pushed her against the wall. "You bitch," he spit out, the rancid smell of whiskey on his breath. "Who in hell do you think you're talking to?"

Abby's heart pounded so hard she thought she might pass out. But she held her ground. "You. Now, I don't think you want to have me scream for help and have everyone know exactly what you really are. So I suggest you let me go."

That did it. Hatred flared in Joel's eyes, but he released her. Abby straightened her dress and turned to leave. She didn't want to give Joel the satisfaction of seeing that he still had power over her. As she made her way down the hall toward the door, Joel's words followed her.

"I wouldn't act so high and mighty, Abby. That rich boyfriend of yours may have bailed you out, but he's just hanging around to rub it in your face."

His accusations goaded her, and she swung around. "Cade's helping me with the ranch."

Joel laughed. "He's helping himself to the ranch. Did you know he paid off the note with his own check?"

Abby felt the blood drain from her face. She swayed. No. She wouldn't believe it. Joel was lying. Cade wouldn't do that to her and Brandon. He wouldn't take everything away.

Ten minutes had passed, and Cade was getting worried. He started down the hall to find Abby, then spotted the reason she'd been detained—Joel Garson. Dammit, couldn't the man leave her alone? When Cade reached him, he grabbed Garson by the collar.

"Don't, Cade," Abby said, and grabbed his arm. "It's okay, I can fight my own battles."

Cade glared at Garson. "I told you to stay away from Abby."

"It's a public place," Joel said. "Besides, like I'd want her. She's all yours, buddy." With a smirk he straightened his shirt. "You think you have it all now, don't you, Randell? Think you're hot stuff, but you're still the son of a cattle rustler. No amount of money or the Moreau land is going to change that."

Cade tensed, seeing the look on Abby's face. So the man couldn't keep his mouth shut. He'd told her about the loan. "You're a drunk, Garson. If I find out you're bothering Abby, I'll come after you."

"You stay out of my way." Joel pushed past him.

Cade went to Abby. "Are you all right?" He reached for her, but she pulled away.

"I'm fine," she said, then walked out of the restaurant. Once they arrived at the truck, Cade opened the door and helped her inside. He hurried around to the other side, knowing he had to explain, and fast. Then, one look at Abby, and he thought it would be best to wait. She needed some time to calm down. Maybe by the time they arrived home, she'd be willing to listen to him.

They arrived twenty minutes later and that didn't happen. As soon as he stopped in the driveway, Abby jumped out of the truck and hurried up the steps into the house.

Cade went after her and followed her into the study. "About what Joel said..." he began.

She swung around and glared at him. "Is it true?"

"It's true, but I only speeded things up. The property couldn't sell fast enough, and Joel was going to foreclose on the ranch."

Abby hadn't been able to stop shaking since she learned the truth. How could Cade do this to her? He'd lied. "You paid off the bank note?"

He nodded and her heart sank lower. She took a breath.

"You own part of the ranch."

"No—yes, technically I do, but that's only until the lakefront property sells. Then I'm not involved at all. It's done all the time in business. There's nothing unethical about the transaction."

She felt the knife go through her. The pain was nearly unbearable. "Except you didn't tell me. And you used your power of attorney to make the deal. Why didn't you include me? Why, Cade? Had you planned this all along? Is this why you came back home? To find a way to take over? Is this payback?"

"No. I only used my money because there wasn't enough time to sell before the deadline on the note.

Since Joel wouldn't give you an extension, I had to do something."

"Show it to me," she demanded. So trusting, she had left all the business matters to him. He'd let her see only what he wanted her to see. When would she learn? She should have handled it herself.

Cade walked to the desk and opened the bottom drawer. He went through several file folders, then pulled out one. He handed it to her. "I was wrong, Abby," he admitted. "I should have told you. But I thought the property would be sold by now."

She opened the file, and the ache in her chest intensified when she saw his name on the second deed. "Did it feel good to see a Moreau so vulnerable, to watch me lose it all?"

Something that looked like pain flashed in his eyes, but she ignored it.

"You haven't lost anything, I made sure of that," he told her. "I never planned to take anything from you, not my son, either."

Abby was beyond listening. "Had you planned this all along—to take over the ranch?"

"No!" he shouted.

She paced. "You know, the ironic thing about this is, you didn't hurt me, Cade. I don't care about this ranch. It was my dad's empire. Funny thing, Brandon loves it, too. So all you've done is hurt your son."

"Dammit, Abby, I wasn't trying to hurt anyone. I was trying to help."

Suddenly another realization hit her. "Oh, God! That was the reason for your marriage proposal. You wanted to make sure you had it all."

"No! You're wrong." He started to move toward her, and she held up her hand.

"I'm through listening to you. And Brandon, he's not going to be hurt because you have a grudge against me. Somehow, some way, I'm going to pay you back." Abby closed her eyes and drew a breath. She couldn't do this anymore. "Now, allow me some dignity and leave."

"How can I? When you think I tried to take the ranch. If you would just let me explain..."

"I know all I need to know."

His eyes turned hard. "This isn't over, Abby. When you calm down, you're going to listen and know that I was only trying to help. I never intended to hurt you."

All her life men had said they knew what was best for her. She soon discovered they only wanted to control her, from her father to Joel. Her husband had gone as far as to use his fists. Well, no more. It had taken her a long time to break away, but she had, and she and Brandon were making a life together.

She should have known better, but when Cade came into her life again, her resolve weakened. She had only thought about love. And all she got was pain. So win or lose the ranch, by God, she was going to do it on her own.

"Goodbye, Cade," she said, then turned away, praying he'd leave before she started crying. As soon as she heard the door close, she broke down. This was the second time she had to send Cade away. The immense pain in her heart told her it wasn't any easier.

Chapter Ten

Cade gripped the steering wheel tighter as he got closer to the Moreau ranch. Nearly two full days had passed since his fight with Abby—since she'd thrown him out. She could be angry with him all she wanted, but she wasn't going to keep him from her.

And Brandon. The boy had to know something was going on. That was probably the reason he'd called and practically begged Cade to come to the house. Well, he wasn't going to be denied his father just because Abby was upset.

Cade pulled into the driveway with the hope that she'd had time to cool off and realize he'd only meant to help. No matter what, Brandon wasn't going to suffer because his parents were having a disagreement.

Cade climbed out of the truck, and Brandon ran out to meet him. He caught the boy as he leaped into his arms. Cade swung him around, listening to the seven-year-old's laughter. Then he set Brandon down.

"Cade, I missed you," the boy said as he reset his cowboy hat on his head.

"I missed you, too."

"Why didn't you come back? You promised."

A lump formed in Cade's throat. He'd hated being away. "I've had some business to take care of, partner. But I'm here now."

"Can we go riding?"

"Sure." They started for the barn. "Is your mother around?"

"Yeah, but she's busy."

Not surprising, Cade thought, knowing he was the last person she wanted to see now. "So it's okay that we go?"

The boy looked up at him with those big brown eyes. "She said it was okay that you take me." Brandon tugged on Cade's arm. "Come on," he coaxed.

Once inside the barn, they wandered down the center aisle, heading toward the tack room. Brandon stood on a bench and took down two bridles from the hooks. Cade grabbed two horse blankets and one of the saddles, then the two of them went into Smoky's stall.

After saddling Brandon's horse, Cade readied a horse for himself. Fifteen minutes later they were riding out the gate, waving goodbye to Charlie.

"Where do you want to go today?"

Brandon smiled. "Mustang Valley?"

"Ah, Brandon, that's a ways out. And it's a pretty hot day." Cade looked up at the cloudless sky. "Wouldn't you like to go to the lake? We can take a swim."

The boy shook his head. "I've never been to the valley. You and Mom have been talking about it. And I never saw a mustang."

Cade started to argue, but he saw the stubborn look on his son's face and changed his mind. Why shouldn't the boy see the valley? "Okay, you're on, but I don't want to hear any complaints when you get tired."

Brandon grinned. "You won't."

"Okay," Cade said as he tugged the reins and nudged his horse west. The boy followed close behind.

"How many mustangs do you think we'll see?" Brandon asked.

"Not sure," Cade replied. "We might not see any."

"I bet we'll see a lot," the boy said as he rode next to his dad. He pulled his hat lower on his head, shading his eyes from the sun. Sitting straight in the saddle, Brandon expertly controlled his horse.

Cade felt such pride he ached to reach over and hug the child who had become so precious to him. Soon, he promised himself. When they got back, he was going to talk to Abby. And nothing would stop him from telling Brandon that he was his father.

Abby fumed as she paced the room. How dare Cade come here and take her son? A rush of panic raced through her, causing her to tremble. What if Cade didn't bring him back?

No. She put the notion out of her head. Cade wouldn't do that. But she knew now that she needed to set some ground rules. Even if she had to go to court to do it. No, she didn't want to do that. But Cade couldn't come here any time he felt like it and take Brandon for a ride.

Suddenly the back door opened, and the sound of voices drifted into the study. Then Brandon and Cade appeared. They were laughing, but when Cade saw her, his smile faded.

"Where have you been?" she asked.

Cade's eyes narrowed. "Out riding," he said.

"Yeah, Mom, Cade took me to Mustang Valley," Brandon said as he rushed to her side. "And I saw them. I saw the ponies."

"Brandon, why didn't you tell me where you were going? You know you're not supposed to go anywhere without permission. I was worried."

The boy stared at his boots. "I forgot."

Abby wanted to pull her son into her arms, but she couldn't. He'd deliberately disobeyed her. "Well, so you won't forget again, you're grounded for the next week. No riding."

Brandon's eyes grew large in shock. "But, Mom…"

Her stern glare cut off his words. "I think you should go to your room now."

Brandon drew a shaky breath, then nodded. He looked at Cade. "Thanks for taking me. Will you come back when I'm off restriction so we can go again?"

Cade hunkered down in front of him. "I'll be back, but I think we need to talk about some rules first."

"I'm sorry, Cade. I didn't mean to get you in trouble." The boy's eyes filmed over with tears. "But when you didn't come to see me yesterday, I thought you were mad and…"

"No, I wasn't angry at you. But I'm upset because you should have told your mother where we were going." He hugged the child. "We'll talk about it later."

Abby turned away until Brandon left the room. When they were finally alone, she swung around to face Cade. Her gaze roamed hungrily over him, taking in his faded jeans and shirt and the battered straw hat in his hand. No longer was there any trace of the Chicago businessman who'd returned home a month ago. Cade Randell looked pure cowboy.

Her eyes met his dark gaze, and she felt herself being drawn to him. She couldn't help but notice the deep lines around his eyes. He hadn't been sleeping. Good, she thought, remembering what he'd done to her. "Just who do you think you are, taking my son without my permission?"

"What are you talking about?" he asked, resting his hands on his hips. "He's my son, too. Besides, you knew I was taking Brandon riding today."

"It would have been common courtesy to check with me."

He blinked in surprise. "I never thought that Brandon would lie. He told me you were busy. I believed him."

Abby nodded and watched the anger drain from Cade's face. "Brandon can be creative when he wants his way."

Cade looked perplexed. "That little stinker."

"And as his mother, I couldn't let him get away with it."

"Listen, Abby, I don't want you to keep my child from me just because we're having a difference of opinion. As you can tell by Brandon's actions, he wants to be with me."

His words hurt her. It was more than a difference of opinion. And Abby had to stick by her decision. Still, why did she have to be the bad guy to her son, while Cade got to do the fun stuff? "You can't want to reward him for lying."

"No, but I want to spend time with him, and you promised you wouldn't stop me."

"And I expect you to ask me first," she complained. "I was terrified when I couldn't find him. Thank goodness Charlie knew he was with you."

"I'm sorry. What more do you want?"

"Just some consideration in the future."

"You got it." His eyes flashed. "And I want something, too. I want to tell Brandon I'm his father."

She shook her head. "No, you can't."

Abby's words pierced his heart. What had he done to deserve this? All he'd wanted was to help save the damn ranch and claim his son. Now she was trying to keep Brandon from him. No more. "I can, and I will. I've waiting long enough for you to decide when, Abby. But you've kept putting it off. Brandon is my son, and it's time he knows I'm his father."

"Please, keep your voice down," Abby begged.

"I've done everything you asked," he said. "I've waited, and I don't know what for."

"Maybe I wouldn't be so suspicious if I felt I could trust you."

Anger flared in him again like a hot coal, and he wanted to shake her. "I never lied to you. All I was trying to do was help. And if you weren't so damn stubborn, you'd understand why, too. But I'm through explaining to you." He started across the room, then stopped at the door. "I *will* tell Brandon I'm his father. So you can expect me back, with a court order if I need it."

He saw the panic in her eyes and regretted the threat. But he had to stand firm. He'd already lost her. But she wasn't going to stand between him and his child.

"Don't do this, Cade. Please. Just wait."

"I've waited nearly eight years, Abby. You have no idea what that's like." His eyes bore into hers. "What I've lost I can never get back. I need my son now, and I believe he needs me."

Cade turned and started out, ignoring Abby's sobs. The sound tore at him, and he wished things could be different. But she wouldn't take the comfort he'd offered. She didn't want any part of him. She never did. And she never would. It had taken him a long time, but he'd finally gotten that through his head.

Cade went back to the Circle B and had dinner with his family, including Chance and Joy. But he couldn't sit around and make pleasant conversation when his mind was on Brandon. Thank goodness Katie held everyone's attention. But for Cade, the baby represented what he had missed with his own child.

He knew realistically he couldn't change things, couldn't turn back the clock, but in his heart, he wished for those years, years he wanted back, not only with Brandon, but with Abby, too. But she didn't want him. She didn't even want Brandon to know he was his father.

Restless, Cade stepped out to the porch just in time to watch the sun disappear in the west. He perched on the railing and stared out toward the large white barn and the corral, deserted now. All the horses had been put away for the night. The entire ranch was quiet. A dog barked off in the distance and the sound of crickets filled the night.

"This sure isn't Chicago," he murmured.

"You gettin' homesick?"

It was Hank. Cade heard the squeak of the porch chair as the older man sat down.

"I thought I *was* home," Cade answered. "Unless you're tired of having me around."

Hank grinned. "Son, I have been happier these past weeks than I've been in years. But I'm not concerned about me. It's you who looks like he's lost his best friend."

Cade closed his eyes and leaned his head against the post. He'd lost more than that. Something much more important. "Abby thinks I'm trying to take the ranch away."

There was a long silence. "Why would she think that?"

"Because I didn't tell her that the bank I acquired to take over her loan was my personal bank, and I'm the cosigner on the new loan." He rushed on. "But if I hadn't done something, Garson was going to foreclose. Now my name is on the second trust deed. But it's only temporary—until I sell the lakefront property."

"And I assume Abby doesn't take kindly to your omission of that detail."

Cade nodded.

"Well, you have to understand," Hank began, "Abby hasn't had much cause to trust men. Her daddy dominated her, just like he did his wife. Never let her think for herself or do anything. He thought he knew what was best for her. Pushed Abby to marry a man he handpicked for her. Then Garson ended up hurting her in ways I'll never understand." Hank sighed. "But you have to give the girl credit—she packed up Brandon and walked away. If she's a little defensive, I expect she has that right."

Cade didn't want to think about what Abby went through during her marriage. "But I wouldn't hurt her."

"I think she knows that deep inside, but every time she's trusted a man, he's let her down."

Suddenly Abby's phone call to him in Chicago flashed through his head. He'd never given her the chance to talk. He'd just told her he didn't love her anymore, then hung up.

He had let her down, too. "What can I do to make her trust me?" he asked.

Hank stood and stretched his arms over his head, then hiked his jeans up high on his narrow waist. "I think you have to figure that one out for yourself." He patted Cade's shoulder. "And when you do, maybe you'll be ready to listen to Abby's reasons for keeping Brandon a secret." The older man turned and went back into the house, leaving Cade alone.

Cade had always thought he was a loner, but being home with his family, especially spending time with Brandon and Abby, he'd learned he didn't want the solitary life. He wanted his son...and Abby.

Suddenly an idea struck him. He might just have a way of convincing her he only wanted her—not the damn ranch. He turned and went inside, more excited than he'd been in days.

The next morning Abby was out of bed and dressed by six after being up and down all night long. Damn Cade Randell, she thought as she entered the kitchen and found Carmen making breakfast.

"Good morning, Abby," the housekeeper said.

Abby walked straight to the coffeepot. "Good morning, Carmen."

She poured herself a mug and took an eager sip. The hot liquid nearly scalded her throat, but it was worth it. Carmen made the best coffee around. Strong and hot. Just what she needed to kickstart her day. Another day without Cade.

She shook away the thought and sat down at the table. Carmen set a plate of eggs and bacon in front of her.

"You eat," the housekeeper ordered. "And no arguing."

"I can't possibly eat all this."

"Then try, and if I think you're making an effort, then I'll excuse you. No man is worth starving yourself for." She patted her own ample hips. "Besides, most men want some meat on a woman's bones." She smiled. "So eat."

Abby stiffened. "I don't need a man."

"You need the *right* man. Then you'd wake up happy, and so would Brandon. So why did you send Mr. Randell away?"

"I had to." Abby's voice softened with emotion. "Believe me, it was for the best."

Carmen shook her head. "Doesn't make sense to me. You're sad all the time, and Brandon, he's been moping around. Who's this best for?"

Abby didn't want to discuss Cade. "I can't handle another loveless marriage. My life with Joel was a disaster. I can't go through that again."

"Mr. Randell would never be like that," the housekeeper said. "I see the way he looks at you and the child. There's only love in his eyes. And with Brandon, he's so gentle, so loving. Even Charlie says so, and you know how protective he is of that boy."

"I know. Charlie has been great with Brandon and

the running of the ranch. I'm so lucky that both of you stayed on.''

"We're here because this is our home, too,'' the older woman said.

Abby thought back over the years and how many times Carmen had been there for her. Like a mother to her, the woman had never judged her for the mistakes she'd made. Even when she'd come back after her failed marriage, Carmen had been there to comfort her and help her heal. They were like family.

With the new developments, Abby didn't know how long she and Brandon could hang on to the ranch. Her pride wouldn't allow her to take charity from Cade.

Carmen came to the table and sat down. She took Abby's hand. "I know times have been rough on you. The men in your life haven't been kind. First your daddy, then that awful Mr. Garson.'' The woman's dark eyes were sad. "You need to know love, Abby. The right way a man should treat a woman. Just don't be afraid to allow that to happen. Give Mr. Randell a chance.''

Tears filled Abby's eyes. She couldn't. She couldn't live with another man who wanted revenge. "I can't. But I can't punish Brandon for my mistakes. Cade was right—our son deserves to know his father.''

Carmen smiled. "That's a start. Just don't keep your heart closed. But I have a feeling that with Mr. Cade Randell that would be difficult.''

Abby knew what Carmen predicted was impossible. She would always love Cade. But she had to be satisfied that he was only in her life because of their son. "It's the way things have to be.''

The housekeeper nodded and stood. "Speaking of Brandon, that boy is still asleep. He's usually up by now. I guess I better go up and see what's keeping him.''

"No, Carmen, I'll go," Abby said. "I need to talk to him. There are some things he needs to know. Things I should have told him a long time ago.'' She walked out into the entry, then up the staircase. On her way down the long hall, she was trying to figure out a way to explain to Brandon about Cade. She knocked, then peeking inside, she called his name.

"Wake up, sleepyhead," she said. Glancing around the room, she soon discovered he wasn't there. His bed had been neatly made, but Brandon was gone. Abby went downstairs and into the kitchen. Picking up the phone, she dialed the barn. When Charlie answered, she asked, "Charlie, is Brandon out there?''

"No, I haven't seen him, but I just got back from town. Hold on, let me check something.'' There was dead air for about thirty seconds, then the foreman came back on the line. "It's what I suspected—Smoky is gone.''

"I'll be right there," Abby said, and hung up. She started for the back door, fear tugging at her heart. "Carmen, I'm going out to look for Brandon. It seems he went riding.''

The housekeeper gasped. "That child has never gone off by himself before.''

"And when I find him, he is oh so restricted.'' Abby wanted to be angry, to deny her fear. Grabbing her hat, she jammed it on her head, knowing she only wanted her son safe. Outside, a gust of wind nearly blew off her hat, but she held it down with one hand as she hurried to the barn.

"Charlie!" she shouted when she got inside.

"I'm back here." The older man came out of the

tack room. "The boy didn't take a saddle, but there's a bridle missing. So he's riding bareback."

Abby's panic rose. "Why? I know he was angry that I restricted him, but he's never openly defied me before. Oh, God. Where did he go? He could be anywhere—I haven't checked on him since last night." She paced the aisle. "I've got to go find him."

"Then we better get started," Charlie advised. "There's a storm coming up." He reached for the phone on the wall. "I'll have Carmen call some of the neighbors to help."

"Call the Circle B and tell Cade that Brand—his son—is missing. And I need him." She hurried into the tack room and grabbed her saddle.

Fifteen minutes later Abby was leading her horse out behind Charlie when a truck came barreling down the road. Cade.

He jumped out and ran toward her. "What's happened to Brandon?"

Tears flooded Abby's eyes as she went to him. "I don't know. He wasn't in bed this morning. And his horse is missing. Oh, Cade, do you think he heard us arguing last night?"

Cade drew her close. "I don't know, Abby. But we're going to find him and we're going to explain—everything."

She nodded and swallowed hard. "You were right, Cade. We should have told him. If he found out by hearing us arguing, he probably thinks..."

He touched her face. "I said we're going to find him. We're not going to let anything happen to him."

"Hey, you two," Charlie interrupted, leading another horse out for Cade. "This weather is going to get worse before it gets better.'' A crash of thunder punctuated his words.

A short time later, protected by rain ponchos, the three rode through the pasture, combing every section for Brandon. The approaching storm was going to bring heavy rain, which could mean trouble for the search. Cade tried to think of all the places he'd taken Brandon, places a kid could hide. But so far, no sign of the boy. An hour had passed, and the rain intensified to a downpour. Chance met up with them just over the rise, but he had nothing to report. He told them he hadn't seen anything as he came from his ranch. Hank arrived a minute later. Even when the group split up, they didn't see any sign of Brandon. And the heavy rain had washed out any signs of a trail.

Cade looked at Abby, and his heart sank into his gut. He wanted desperately to relieve the fear he saw in her eyes. The fear he felt himself but didn't show. He had to find their son.

''Abby, you're shaking,'' he said, knowing the temperature had dropped fifteen degrees. ''You should go back to the house and wait. Hank and I will continue the search.''

''No. I'm staying until we find Brandon.''

''Maybe we should call in the sheriff,'' Hank suggested.

''It would take another hour before they got here,'' Cade said. ''I'd rather call in more of the neighbors. They'd get here faster.''

Hank pulled out his cell phone and punched in some numbers. While he was talking, an idea came to Cade. ''I think I know where Brandon might have gone. Mustang Valley.''

The rain made the ride slow going, but when Cade,

Abby and Hank crested the hill and looked down into the valley, they found the gray mare under a tree. Filled with hope, they rode to the creek, all three hollering for Brandon.

Then Cade heard a faint cry. He jumped off his horse and hurried around the shrubs toward a group of trees. He found a shivering Brandon huddled under a low branch, trying to stay dry. "I found him," he yelled to the others, then rushed to the boy's side. When he picked him up, the soaked child clung to his neck and began to cry.

"Cade," he said, "I was so scared."

"It's okay, Brandon." Cade hugged him close. "I'm here, and I'm not leaving you."

Abby rushed over to her son. Hank jumped off his mount, too, and slipped a rain poncho over the boy's head and pulled the hood up.

"We need to get the boy out of this weather," Hank said. "There's a lineman shack about half a mile from here. If I remember, Tom kept it in good shape."

Cade agreed they should head there and he carried Brandon to his horse. Ten minutes later they arrived at the one-room structure. Tying up the horses under the covered porch and out of the rain, Hank pushed open the door and ushered everyone inside.

He glanced around the sparsely furnished room until he saw what he wanted. "Good, there's dry wood." The older man pulled off his rain-slicked poncho and went to the fireplace. Within minutes he had a fire going. Within moments the room began to warm.

Brandon's teeth chattered. "I'm s-so c-cold."

"I know, son." Cade had pulled off his poncho and now did the same for Brandon. Then he began to strip off the boy's wet clothes. Once he was down to his underwear, Cade put him in front of the fire.

Abby dried his hair with a blanket from a shelf of meager supplies. She looked at Cade and mouthed the words, *thank you*. He nodded, but wanted more from her than gratitude. He wanted to take her in his arms and tell her how he felt about her and Brandon. But she didn't want him, so instead, with his emotions raw, he turned and walked out the door to the porch.

Hank was taking care of the horses. "I called home and let them know where we are," he said. "Chance is gonna bring the truck when the rain lets up."

"Thanks." Cade began to tremble, and he couldn't seem to stop. "I thought we'd lost him." Tears filled his eyes. "I didn't think we were going to find him...safe."

Hank crossed to Cade and pulled him into a strong embrace. "He's fine now, son. Everything is fine. You've got to find out why he ran away. Something like that doesn't happen without a reason."

Cade pulled away. "I think he overheard Abby and I arguing."

"Then if that's true, you need to straighten things out."

"I don't know what to say." He looked at Hank pleadingly. "I would have been there if I'd known about my son. I would have married his mother. I loved her."

"Tell him that," Hank suggested. "And don't leave out that Abby loved you, too."

Cade stared out at the rain sheeting off the edge of the porch. "How can you say that?"

"Because it's true." Hank raised an eyebrow.

"Over the years, did you ever ask yourself why Abby changed her mind about you so quickly?"

Cade hated thinking about that time. "I just figured she let her daddy talk her out of it."

He nodded. "That part is true. But there was more. A few years ago I learned what Tom Moreau did that day. It seems that when Abby told her daddy that she was in love and was engaged to marry you, he had a fit and ordered her to break it off. Abby refused. Then Tom pulled out his big guns. He told his daughter about some robberies on the ranch and that two of his men saw you in the area." Hank studied Cade for a long moment. "Tom told her that these men would testify against you in court if she didn't break it off with you."

Cade was having trouble believing the story. But he wouldn't put anything past Tom Moreau. "I never stole anything from him."

"I know that, and Abby knew it, too," Hank continued. "But she thought she needed to keep you safe, so she had to let you go." Hank cleared his throat. "She did it because she loved you, Cade."

He felt as if he'd been punched in the chest. He couldn't breathe, remembering the phone call. "Oh, God." He wiped a hand over his face. "I never gave her the chance to tell me she was pregnant."

"You both made mistakes," Hank added. "You were young. I think it's time you both forgave each other." He nodded to the cabin. "You have a child who needs you."

Inside the cabin, Abby hugged Brandon to her and pulled the blanket tighter. His trembling had finally stopped, and he was asleep now. She was tired, too, but she wasn't going to leave her son.

The door opened and Cade came in. She drew a breath at the sight of him. He was so handsome and she loved him, even more after watching how he'd handled things today. He crossed to her and sat down.

"I'm sorry," he whispered, and looked at his sleeping son. "I'm sorry I caused so much trouble."

She shook her head. "No, I'm the one who's sorry, Cade. I should never have kept your son from you. I was just so scared he would hate me." She stopped and blinked, praying she wouldn't cry. "He needs you, Cade. You've been so good with him."

"Brandon could never hate you, Abby." Cade's hand touched her arm, and she felt his warmth. "My son is lucky to have you for his mother. You were just protecting him. Just like you've protected all the people you love. Can you forgive me for being a first-class jerk?"

"We both were acting crazy," she admitted, cuddling her son against her body. "I was so afraid all you wanted was to get even with me for keeping you from Brandon."

Cade stroked his son's head and accidentally touched her breast. His eyes shot to hers, and she saw desire flame in the dark depths. "We need to talk about some things, Abby." Brandon stirred in her arms. "Later."

Brandon opened his eyes and looked at Cade. "Are you mad at me?"

"Not at this moment." Cade smiled "I'm too happy you're safe. But you have a lot of explaining to do, son. Like why you went riding by yourself."

The boy's eyes traveled from Cade to Abby. "'Cause you and Mom were fighting...about me. I didn't want to make any more trouble." Tears formed in his eyes. "I remember when my dad used to fight with Mom about me. He didn't like me."

"I'm not like Joel."

The boy nodded. "I know. You never get mad and yell. But I still got scared. I remembered you said that you used to go to Mustang Valley when you needed to think about things. You said you always felt better being there. You didn't feel like a misfit. I needed to think about things, too. I was okay, but when it started to rain... I tried to wait until it stopped, but it didn't." The boy's eyes met his. "I was hoping you'd come after me. Are you really my dad, like you said back at the house?"

Cade's heart swelled with love. "Yes, I'm your dad," he said.

Brandon's eyes widened. "Oh, boy. I used to pretend you were. Do you love me?"

"Oh, yes, I love you. I love you very much."

Brandon nearly jumped in his arms and hugged him. "I love you, too...Dad."

Cade hung on tight. Nothing had ever felt this good. He looked at Abby. Only one thing would make it perfect.

The boy pulled back. "Does that mean my name is Brandon Randell?"

"Would you like that?"

"I'd like that a lot." He wrinkled his nose. "But what about my mom? Will she be a Randell, too?"

Chapter Eleven

Cade wanted to tell his son the truth. That with all his heart he wished Abby would take his name so they could be a family. But before he could get the words out, the sound of Chance's truck horn distracted everyone.

"Looks like our ride is here," Hank announced as he peered in the doorway.

"I don't have any clothes on," Brandon said, grabbing his blanket.

"That's the reason we have to get you home," Cade said as he swung his son up in his arms. "You'll be wrapped up, so no one will see your bare bottom."

Brandon laughed as Chance walked in, wiping the rain from his coat. His gaze shot to Brandon and he grinned. "Hey, isn't it a little wet for a ride?"

The boy smiled shyly. "I didn't know it was going to rain."

"Yeah, who would have thought in the middle of a

drought we'd get a gully-washer." Chance turned serious. "Hey, kid, you had a lot of people worried."

"I know. I'm sorry."

"That's okay, you had a lot on your mind," he said, patting the boy's arm. "Sometimes a man's got to get away and think things out."

Brandon studied Chance. "Are you my uncle?"

Cade's older brother paused, then nodded. "Yeah, I'm your uncle."

"Cool," the boy said. "I never had an uncle before."

"Well, I never had a nephew, either," Chance countered. "Now I think we better get you home. We'll have a family get-together soon."

Cade started out the door with his son. "Chance, if you'll take Abby and Brandon back to the house, I'll stay and bring back the horses."

"I can stay with Hank," Chance offered. "You drive your family back."

Cade liked the sound of that. "You sure?" he asked.

Chance nodded and leaned closer. "Take it from someone who knows—they both need you now."

Cade's hold on his son tightened. "Okay, I owe you."

"Believe me, I'm going to collect," Chance said. "Now go." He shoved them toward the door. "Abby, we'll make sure the horses get back."

"Thanks, Chance," she said.

They walked out to the porch. The rain had slowed considerably. Fragments of blue sky showed that the storm was moving on. "Thanks, brother," Cade said. "And, Hank…" He couldn't think of words to express his gratitude.

"Anytime, son. I couldn't lose my grandson."

"Wow." Brandon's eyes lit up. "I got a grandfather, too!"

"Just calm down," Abby said. "You're going to have to be punished, so it'll be a while before you see any relatives."

"You're going to punish me?"

Abby smiled. "No. I'm going to let your dad do that."

Cade groaned. "Great. Guess it's my turn to be the bad guy."

"Get used to it," she said. "It's all part of the job."

Cade leaned toward her. "I'm still going to love being a daddy." Before she could say anything else, he hustled Brandon into the truck and fastened him inside before Abby arrived. Cade took the same care with her and saw that she was safely in her seat. Then with a wave, he jumped in, started the engine and headed home with his precious cargo.

Fifteen minutes later they were back at the ranch, where Charlie and Carmen were waiting with open arms. By the time Brandon had a bath and was tucked in bed, Cade could see he was pretty sick of all the attention.

"Hey, don't knock it," Cade told him. "Someday you'll love having a woman give you so much attention."

"Mom and Carmen treat me like a baby."

"Well, I wish I'd had a mother like yours. Mine died when I was about your age."

"Oh. Who took care of you?"

"My brothers and I went to live on the Circle B. Ella was like a mother to me. She was great."

"Then will she be like my grandmother?"

Cade couldn't help but grin, knowing the matronly housekeeper's love for kids. "She would like that. Boy, you are going to get spoiled."

Brandon looked pleased at himself, then slowly his expression changed. "Are you going to marry my mom?"

Cade had wondered how long it would take before that question came up, but he was still caught off guard. He sat down on the bed and leaned back against the headboard, then pulled his son to him. "That's a tough question, son. So much has happened between your mom and me. So many years. There are things you won't understand until you're older…"

"I'm older now," he insisted. "I know my grandpa didn't like you. Is he the reason you didn't marry my mom?"

Cade didn't want Brandon to have any hard feelings toward his grandfather. "That's one of the reasons, but he thought he was doing what was best for your mom," he said truthfully, watching his son yawn. "Now, I think you might need some sleep."

"I'm not tired," Brandon said as his eyelids drifted shut. "Please don't leave me."

"I'm here, son." Cade brushed the boy's hair from his forehead, determined to somehow straighten things out with Abby. "I'm not going anywhere."

Abby carried the food tray back downstairs, after overhearing the father and son's conversation. With Cade promising Brandon that he wasn't going anywhere, she decided to let them have some time and privacy.

Feeling a little jealous of their closeness, she headed

back to the kitchen and dropped off the tray. She found Ella and Joy seated at the table.

"They didn't want anything to eat?" Ella asked.

Abby shook her head. "Brandon's nearly asleep, and I didn't want to disturb them."

"You're Brandon's mother—you can disturb them all you want," Ella said, and pushed a bag across the table. "Here, I brought some clean clothes for Cade. Will you see that he gets them?"

Abby nodded, but knew she couldn't face Cade now. Not after everything that had happened. They'd come so close to losing Brandon. And it was her fault. She should have let Cade tell Brandon he was his father long ago.

Joy came around the table to Abby. "What's the matter?"

Abby sighed. "Nothing. Just some leftover emotions from the day's events. I'll be fine."

She walked out of the kitchen, hoping no one would follow her. Before she made it upstairs to her room, there was a knock on the front door. Abby went to answer it. On the porch she found an express-mail-service driver.

"Good afternoon, ma'am. Sorry for the delay. The storm left us behind schedule." He handed her a large envelope. "Would you sign here, please?"

Abby wrote out her signature on the clipboard, then handed it back to the driver. She shut the door and walked into the study as she examined the envelope. The return name was that of a local bank. She ripped off the tape and pulled out a manila folder. Inside she found a sheaf of papers. She scanned the first page, then the next, until she realized that what she was reading was the second deed to the ranch. The name on the deed was Brandon Garson Randell. Cade had transferred it from his own name to his son's. Abby's breath caught, then stopped completely. Her name was there as trustee of the account.

She sank onto the sofa. Cade had been telling her the truth. All this time he was doing what he said he was doing—helping.

She glanced down at the folder and found a note attached:

Abby, I hope this will clear up any misunderstandings. My only intention was to help. Everything I did was for our son. I should have told you. I'm sorry. Can you forgive me?

Cade

Tears formed in her eyes as she crushed the letter to her chest. "Can you forgive *me?*" she said, remembering all the things she'd accused him of.

She had to set things straight. She had to let Cade know she'd been wrong. She went upstairs and opened the door to her son's bedroom. She saw father and son both sound asleep on the bed.

With her heart in her throat, she walked to the side of the bed, her gaze hungry for the two most important people in her life. She watched the slow even rise and fall of Cade's chest. One large protective arm was around his son. A tear slid down her cheek. Brandon should have had this all his life. Her back stiffened as she brushed the moisture from her face. Somehow she was going to make sure that Brandon knew his father.

Abby leaned down and kissed her son's forehead. She ached to touch Cade, but was afraid. What right did she have? "Oh, Cade, I'm so sorry," she whispered, then turned and walked out.

Not wanting to talk to anyone, Abby went to her room and showered away the grime of the day. She wasn't interested in any dinner, and deciding to let Cade handle Brandon's needs, she went to bed.

But hours later she still couldn't find the peace of sleep. She finally got up and went to check on Brandon. He was still safely asleep in his bed. Alone. Disappointed, she realized Cade must have gone home. Probably a good thing. She wasn't ready to face him. She wandered downstairs into the study. Not turning on any lights, she sat down on the sofa and let the moonlight wash over her.

"Why didn't you tell me?"

Abby gasped. Her gaze shot toward the sound of Cade's voice, and she saw him standing in the shadows next to the desk. "Cade!"

"Why, Abby?" he asked again as he stepped out into the moonlight. "Why almost eight years ago did you let me walk away?"

Her heart pounding, she took in his appearance. He had changed into a clean pair of faded jeans and dark polo shirt, which stretched over his broad chest, wide shoulders and muscular arms. Arms that had held her so tenderly, their son so protectively. She forced her attention back to the question. "It doesn't matter now, Cade."

"It does matter, Abby. Did you think I would let your daddy stop us?" he asked, his face contorted in pain. "We loved each other. And all this time it was Tom Moreau keeping you from me. Did you know that for years I thought you didn't love me?" His gaze revealed the hurt she'd caused him. "Why didn't you trust me?"

Tears formed in her eyes as she realized he'd found out about her father's threats. "He said he would have you put in jail."

Cade walked across the room. In the dim light she could see his drawn look. "I would have chanced it," he said. "It would have been worth it, to be with you." His words spread warmth through her. He reached out and took her hand, then pulled her to her feet. "I would have done anything to have you," he whispered. Then he placed a tender kiss against her mouth. Abby ached to have his arms around her forever.

"Anything," he whispered.

"But—"

He kissed her again, stopping her resistance. "No more arguing. It doesn't matter anymore, Abby. We're going to forget the past—no more assigning blame. We're together now. You, me and Brandon. You're going to marry me."

Abby wanted to say yes. But she wanted his love, not simply a promise to make a family for their son. She pulled away, needing to distance herself from him.

"Cade, we have to talk," she said.

Cade felt a sense of panic the second Abby left his arms. He ached to go to her, to force her into admitting her feelings. She seemed like a dream as she paced the moon-washed room in her flowing gown, the gossamer material moving against her willowy frame, her hair free and wild.

He swallowed back his groan. "Go ahead," he said. "Talk."

She sighed. "First I want to tell you I'm sorry for

overreacting about the loan. I know now that you were only trying to help us. I got the deed in the mail this afternoon. Thank you.''

"No, I was wrong. I should have told you what I had in mind. But time and lack of options prevented it.''

"Still, Cade, I knew you were a decent man and weren't going to run off with my money.''

"But there was just a moment when you thought that I wanted to get even with you for not telling me about Brandon.''

She nodded. "Guilty. But I hoped you wouldn't do that. You were trying to help. You see, it had taken me so long to regain control of my life.'' She swallowed. "I was worried that I would begin to depend on you too much.''

"And this is a bad thing?''

"It is when I have to move on,'' she said.

Cade was trying to understand her logic, but knowing the men in her past, it suddenly dawned on him. "Abby, I'm not your father or Joel. I want to be your partner, your husband, your lover.''

"You say that now, but what happens when you can't stay married to me because you've found someone you...you love?''

"Abby, you can't believe that I'd ever...'' Oh, God, he understood now. She didn't think he loved her. He went to her and took her hands, making her look at him.

"Abby, I'll never find anyone else. There has never *been* anyone else. For as long as I can remember I've been in love with you. I loved you when you were sixteen, and I love you now.''

Her beautiful green eyes widened. "You still love me?"

He nodded. "Now, to make this the most perfect day of my life, you could tell me how you feel about me." He held his breath.

"Oh, Cade, I love you so much." She went into his arms, her body trembling with sobs.

"Oh, baby, I've waited so long for you to say those words. Just stop crying."

She did as she pulled away. "I thought you hated me."

"Anger was my only defense against you," he admitted. "When I saw you at Hank's party, I still wanted you, but I had to lash out so I wouldn't give away my real feelings." He shuddered. "When I think about the things I've said to you…when all those years you were only protecting me." He reached for her. "I love you. I really love you."

Abby wrapped her arms around his waist. "Every day all I had to do was look at our son, and I saw you. In his eyes, in his smile. I couldn't stop loving you." She pulled back and searched his face. "We've lost so much. I wish—"

"Shh," he whispered. "No more regrets. We're together now. That is, if you'll marry me."

Abby smiled through her tears. "Oh, yes. I'll marry you, Cade Randell."

Cade's mouth covered hers in a hungry kiss. He pulled her against him, her heart against his, beating with his. He had his Abby back, but he had so much more. He had his family.

He broke off the kiss. "We better go upstairs and tell our son that his mother is going to have the same last name."

Abby resisted his nudge. "Whoa, Mr. Randell, you have a lot to learn. You never wake up children. If you do—" her arms moved up his chest and around his neck "—Mom and Dad will never have time to themselves. And we definitely need time alone."

Cade smiled. "And we definitely have a lot of time to make up." He kissed her until they were both thinking about something other than their child.

"Oh, you are a fast learner, Cade Randell."

"I'm completely in your hands, Mrs. Soon-to-be Randell." He captured her lips again and began to wash away the memory of all the empty years they'd spent apart. Because it didn't matter anymore. The future was theirs. Together.

Epilogue

In Mustang Valley, Cade stood beside his bay gelding, gazing at his wife of six weeks. Abby Randell looked as beautiful in her faded jeans, fitted western shirt and straw cowboy hat as she had when she'd walked down the aisle in her ivory wedding dress.

The quiet ceremony had been held just two weeks after the night he proposed, with only family and a few friends present. Then, Hank and Ella hosted a reception at the Circle B. Cade's favorite part was the five-day honeymoon in the Bahamas. With the promise of Disney World over Christmas break, Brandon stayed with his new grandfather, Hank, while Mom and Dad flew off to paradise. Cade needed to concentrate on his bride. And he did. Taking long walks on the beach, they erased their years apart and got to know each other all over again. Then there had been the incredible nights in each other's arms, the love-making. Afterward they planned their future with Brandon and talked of having more children.

Cade sighed. Being home had been equally wonderful. He'd moved in to the Moreau ranch. But once the ranch was turned into a working guest ranch, he wanted to build a home closer to the valley. And he knew just the spot. It would take a few years, but he didn't mind the wait. Not when he had Abby. And his son.

He glanced at his wife, watching her temper flare as she tried to get her point across to the construction foreman. Cade smiled. Maybe it was time to rescue the man.

Cade led the horses to one of the new cabins. "Abby, I think we should get back to the house. I promised Brandon we'd finish building the fort this afternoon."

"In a minute, Cade," she said. "Just as soon as Mr. Reed understands that I need larger windows in the cabin, just like I ordered."

Cade pushed back his hat and looked at the foreman. "I'm sure Mr. Reed will fix it."

"It will take longer to get the reorder in," the foreman explained.

Abby placed her hands on her hips. "Then do it. And ship them express." She smiled sweetly. "You have two weeks to finish the job the way we agreed, or the guests will be staying at your house, Mr. Reed."

Cade took Abby's hand. "Good day, Mr. Reed," he said, and tugged his wife with him.

Once back at their mounts, Abby pulled away. "I forgot to tell him something."

Cade stopped her. "It can wait until tomorrow." He kissed her. "I can't. I'm in need of a little TLC."

Abby finally smiled. "Oh, you poor baby. What

about last night?'' She raised an eyebrow. ''And this morning?''

''That was hours ago,'' Cade complained. ''Besides, we have two hours until Brandon comes home from the Circle B.''

''So you've shipped our son off so you can have your way with me.''

''A lot of good it's doing way out here in the middle of a construction site.''

''Well, I guess we had better take care of that.'' Abby gave him that special look, then mounted her horse. ''Hope you can keep up with me,'' she said, then kicked her horse into a gallop.

Cade loved her teasing and the challenge. He got on his gelding and rode after her. It took him a while to catch up, but he finally got Abby to slow down, and they walked the animals.

''You know, we're pretty lucky,'' he told her. ''I almost feel guilty.''

''How can you say that? We had to go through so much to get here. I think we deserve every bit of our happiness.'' She stretched in the saddle. ''And once we get the retreat open next month, I'll be able to start paying you back for the loan.''

Cade started to protest when he caught her smile. He knew Abby would always need her independence. But before the wedding, they'd formed a partnership for the Moreau ranch. The money Cade had invested to cover the loan was now reinvested in the guest retreat. Cade might have started out trying to save his son's inheritance, but it turned out that Abby and Brandon had saved him.

''I think I'd like to renegotiate those terms,'' he said.

Abby's green eyes deepened, as did her voice. "Maybe I should take you back to my office and show you what I want. Think you have a little time to spare?"

Cade felt his body temperature rise. "Lady, for what I have in mind, it's going to take a long time."

"Mmm, I like the sound of that."

"You're going to like a lot more," he promised as he smacked her horse's rump and kicked his own animal into a gallop. Their pace didn't slow until they reached the barn. Charlie had one of the new ranch hands take the horses as Cade and Abby headed to the house. They were both laughing by the time they reached the porch.

"I love you, Mr. Randell."

He kissed her. "And I love you, Mrs. Randell. Give me a few minutes, and I'll show you how much." He backed her against the door. He knew how lucky they were, not only because they loved each other, but because they'd found what they'd lost. "And I plan to show you for the rest of our lives."

His mouth claimed hers just as a vehicle started down the road to the ranch, kicking up dust in its wake. Cade kept his arm around Abby and watched as a late-model truck stopped out front and the door opened.

Travis Randell stepped out into the sunlight. The look on his younger brother's face told Cade there was trouble.

They both rushed to greet him. "Hey, Trav, it's about time you came home." Cade hugged him.

"Sorry. I guess I should have called." His face looked weary, his eyes sad.

"You never need to call. You're always welcome. Any special reason you're here now?"

Travis's eyes went from Cade to Abby, then he exhaled a long breath and said, "I need my family."

Cade tightened his grip around his wife's waist. So his brother had finally found his way back. "The Randells stick together." He smiled. "Welcome home, Travis."

* * * * *

Don't miss

TRAVIS COMES HOME (#1530)

by Patricia Thayer
in July 2001 in
Silhouette Romance!

SILHOUETTE® MAKES YOU A STAR!

Feel like a star with Silhouette.

We will fly you and a guest to New York City for an exciting weekend stay at a glamorous 5-star hotel. Experience a refreshing day at one of New York's trendiest spas and have your photo taken by a professional. Plus, receive $1,000 U.S. spending money!

Flowers...long walks...dinner for two... how does Silhouette Books make romance come alive for you?

Send us a script, with 500 words or less, along with visuals (only drawings, magazine cutouts or photographs or combination thereof). Show us how Silhouette Makes Your Love Come Alive. Be creative and have fun. No purchase necessary. All entries must be clearly marked with your name, address and telephone number. All entries will become property of Silhouette and are not returnable. **Contest closes September 28, 2001.**

Please send your entry to: **Silhouette Makes You a Star!**

In U.S.A.
P.O. Box 9069
Buffalo, NY, 14269-9069

In Canada
P.O. Box 637
Fort Erie, ON, L2A 5X3

Look for contest details on the next page, by visiting www.eHarlequin.com or request a copy by sending a self-addressed envelope to the applicable address above. Contest open to Canadian and U.S. residents who are 18 or over. Void where prohibited.

Silhouette®
Where love comes alive™

Our lucky winner's photo will appear in a Silhouette ad. Join the fun!

SRMYAS1

HARLEQUIN "SILHOUETTE MAKES YOU A STAR!" CONTEST 1308
OFFICIAL RULES
NO PURCHASE NECESSARY TO ENTER

1. To enter, follow directions published in the offer to which you are responding. Contest begins June 1, 2001, and ends on September 28, 2001. Entries must be postmarked by September 28, 2001, and received by October 5, 2001. Enter by hand-printing (or typing) on an 8 ½" x 11" piece of paper your name, address (including zip code), contest number/name and attaching a script containing <u>500 words or less, along with drawings, photographs or magazine cutouts, or combinations thereof</u> (i.e., collage) <u>on no larger than 9" x 12"</u> piece of paper, describing how the <u>Silhouette books make romance come alive for you.</u> Mail via first-class mail to: Harlequin "Silhouette Makes You a Star!" Contest 1308, (in the U.S.) P.O. Box 9069, Buffalo, NY 14269-9069, (in Canada) P.O. Box 637, Fort Erie, Ontario, Canada L2A 5X3. Limit one entry per person, household or organization.

2. Contests will be judged by a panel of members of the Harlequin editorial, marketing and public relations staff. Fifty percent of criteria will be judged against script and fifty percent will be judged against drawing, photographs and/or magazine cutouts. Judging criteria will be based on the following:

   * Sincerity—25%
   * Originality and Creativity—50%
   * Emotionally Compelling—25%

   In the event of a tie, duplicate prizes will be awarded. Decisions of the judges are final.

3. All entries become the property of Torstar Corp. and may be used for future promotional purposes. Entries will not be returned. No responsibility is assumed for lost, late, illegible, incomplete, inaccurate, nondelivered or misdirected mail.

4. Contest open only to residents of the U.S. (except Puerto Rico) and Canada who are 18 years of age or older, and is void wherever prohibited by law; all applicable laws and regulations apply. Any litigation within the Province of Quebec respecting the conduct or organization of a publicity contest may be submitted to the Régie des alcools, des courses et des jeux for a ruling. Any litigation respecting the awarding of a prize may be submitted to the Régie des alcools, des courses et des jeux only for the purpose of helping the parties reach a settlement. Employees and immediate family members of Torstar Corp. and D. L. Blair, Inc., their affiliates, subsidiaries and all other agencies, entities and persons connected with the use, marketing or conduct of this contest are not eligible to enter. Taxes on prizes are the sole responsibility of the winner. Acceptance of any prize offered constitutes permission to use winner's name, photograph or other likeness for the purposes of advertising, trade and promotion on behalf of Torstar Corp., its affiliates and subsidiaries without further compensation to the winner, unless prohibited by law.

5. Winner will be determined no later than November 30, 2001, and will be notified by mail. Winner will be required to sign and return an Affidavit of Eligibility/Release of Liability/Publicity Release form within 15 days after winner notification. Noncompliance within that time period may result in disqualification and an alternative winner may be selected. All travelers must execute a Release of Liability prior to ticketing and must possess required travel documents (e.g., passport, photo ID) where applicable. Trip must be booked by December 31, 2001, and completed within one year of notification. No substitution of prize permitted by winner. Torstar Corp. and D. L. Blair, Inc., their parents, affiliates and subsidiaries are not responsible for errors in printing of contest, entries and/or game pieces. In the event of printing or other errors that may result in unintended prize values or duplication of prizes, all affected game pieces or entries shall be null and void. **Purchase or acceptance of a product offer does not improve your chances of winning.**

6. Prizes: (1) Grand Prize—A 2-night/3-day trip for two (2) to New York City, including round-trip coach air transportation nearest winner's home and hotel accommodations (double occupancy) at The Plaza Hotel, a glamorous afternoon makeover at <u>a trendy New York spa</u>, $1,000 in U.S. spending money and an opportunity to <u>have a professional photo taken and appear in a Silhouette advertisement</u> (approximate retail value: $7,000). (10) Ten Runner-Up Prizes of gift packages (retail value $50 ea.). Prizes consist of only those items listed as part of the prize. Limit one prize per person. Prize is valued in U.S. currency.

7. For the name of the winner (available after December 31, 2001) send a self-addressed, stamped envelope to: Harlequin "Silhouette Makes You a Star!" Contest 1197 Winners, P.O. Box 4200 Blair, NE 68009-4200 or you may access the www.eHarlequin.com Web site through February 28, 2002.

Contest sponsored by Torstar Corp., P.O Box 9042, Buffalo, NY 14269-9042.